A
Sweet
Taste
IN YOUR MOUTH

BY

ANAYA KAY

ISBN: 0989516415

ISBN 13: 9780989516419

To slow sips, good reads, and
friends...the family we choose.

Acknowledgements

Wow! This book is a work of fiction. I can't believe this book is finally completed, after so many challenges, changes, and adventures. Thank you to my readers. I am so grateful for you blessing me with your time and money by purchasing *A Sweet Taste in Your Mouth*. This project was able to come to completion with the help of many people. I would like to thank my parents and family for their support and encouragement, especially through my rejections. The positive feedback truly helped me when facing so many letters. Thank you to the ladies of Brown Sugah Travel Club … especially Dawn, Mel, and Key for reading every version of this book. Yes, I am aware you are tired of these characters and feel like they are a part of you. Thank you to my two male voices, Ron and Al, for reading through the various versions of this book and providing your feedback as men. Thank you to Dr. Elliott Evans for reading a very ruff book and pointing out, "Hey you have a natural voice". Thank you to Lori for reading this book and supporting me through the publishing process. Thank you to Clarence Nero for giving me the opportunity to meet and converse with giants in the literary world. The Bayou Soul Writer's and Readers Conference is a wonderful place to learn. Thank you to Ms. Anita Bunkley for her editorial advice and for encouraging my voice as a young writer. Finally, to my readers, I hope this book and my future books give you an opportunity to laugh, have fun, and slow sip. In New Orleans we believe in a little something extra, please enjoy the drink menu and discussion questions with your friends. Happy Reading~~Anaya

Caramelized Crème Candy

K nock, knock, knock.

"Oh, my, what a great surprise! I was just leaving for Snug's," said Candy.

"Are you going tonight?" said Shane.

Candy stared at the man in front of her. He put fine in fine. Too bad he was out of luck tonight. "Yep, it's Thursday and Thursday equals Snug's with the girlies. What's up Caramel Crème?" she asked, using the nickname she'd given Shane.

"I wanted to spend some time and just share my love for you. You know, have some quality time," said Caramel Crème.

"Well, it's Thursday. Shouldn't you be with your fiancé?" said Candy.

"No, she's out with her moms and I wanted to spend some time with my woman."

"Ha-Ha! Now I'm your woman when another woman wears your ring. Look, step back. I'm trying to lock my door."

"Is that right?" said Caramel Crème.

"Man, please back up and move out of my way," said Candy.

"Come on now. Don't do a brotha like that."

Candy questioned sarcastically, "Do an engaged brotha like what?"

"You want to let me in and give me some of that good, good Candy?" said Caramel Crème.

"Some of that what?" she blushed.

Candy looked Caramel Crème up and down, from his black crocodile laced-up Belvedere shoes to his Steve Harvey tailored suit, and stared at the growing bulge where the stitch of the crotch met the zipper. She said to herself, "Damn. I'm moist already."

"I can show you better than I can tell you," said Caramel Crème.

"Well, guess what? You are going to have to show me at another time. Look this is really not a good time. We have our set rendezvous day and you have canceled over and over again. So, you have no one to fault but yourself. So, could you please take your arms from around me? I am going to be late," she said.

"You know I have been busy. C'mon. Mr. Colossal's been craving for some of that ushy, gushy candy," Caramel begged.

"Ha-Ha! We got jokes. I know your moves, and your moves need to be saved up for your woman when she gets back from kicking with her moms," said Candy.

"What's that?" said Caramel Crème.

"What's what, Mr. Crème? That is my cell phone vibrating."

"Oh I can make you vibrate just like that phone," said Caramel Crème.

"Look, got to go. That's my girls. I'm late and they are probably at Snug's holding it down waiting on me," said Candy.

"Come on, Candy. Give a brother some play. You know how much we love each other. Deep down inside, you want me just as much as I want you." Whispering in her ear, he said, "Don't you like your colossal dick anymore? You know every time I hit that, you sing about its powers," said Caramel Crème.

Candy dissed Caramel Crème's flirtations with a wave of her hand.

"Look, I got to go," she mumbled. "Don't you hear my phone vibrating? And my girls are waiting. It's time for me to bop da bop up out of here, and besides, you have someone who can give you all of what you need, isn't that what the ring means? You have found the woman who fulfills all your dreams and sexual fantasies, right? Look, I got to go."

"Come on, Candy. What about a quickie to take the edge off?" Caramel Crème asked, still begging.

"All right, look twenty-five minutes in and out and not a minute more. I must make it to Snug's to kick it. Come on in, have a seat on the sofa. Don't look toward my bedroom cause you ain't getting in my bed. I might love your ass, but you don't love me. We can do this on the sofa or the floor. My bed, from now on, is for my prince, the one who is going to give me a ring."

"Cool, baby, let's do this," said Caramel Crème.

Candy went to the guest bathroom and removed her straight fitting, hip hugging Prada black dress. She smiled at her curvaceous figure in the mirror, winking at herself. "Damn girl, you are looking too sweet in that

Victoria Secret red lace panty set with Jimmy Choo four-inch, red snakeskin heels. Mirror, Mirror on the wall who's the sexiest Candy?" she flirted with the mirror.

"Let me take that off of you, baby. Keep the shoes on, baby. You know I like to fuck you with them fancy shoes on," he said.

"Take it slow, baby, don't rip my lace," she whispered.

"Oh, yeah. I am going to take my time," Caramel Crème assured her.

Candy sat down on the sofa with her legs wide open and began biting her bottom lip as Caramel Crème started to undress. Waiting anxiously, she rubbed and pinched her nipples and began to gyrate slowly, in a circular motion, as Colossal came out of his cage. Caramel Crème began to stroke Colossal as it grew from eight inches to ten.

"Tell me something," Candy began.

"Yeah baby," he asked.

"How many licks will it take until you get to middle?" Candy spread her vagina lips to expose her pink, hardened clit.

"Damn baby. Not long; not long at all," he assured her.

"Well, show me," said Candy as she waited for Colossal.

Candy loved to go on fantastic riding expeditions. Pulling her hair back into a ponytail, saying in a whispering tone, "Thank yah, Jesus, thank yah." During their regular times together, Candy would take her lovely time, starting slowly, with juicy filled licks and kisses that gave her lips a shine—as if she were wearing lip-gloss. Knowing time was not on her side, Candy grabbed Colossal and wrapped both hands around it. Thinking to herself, before she tasted Colossal's juices, *"I thought you belonged to another, but from the way you growing for me it's going to be a good night."* Candy licked and sucked Colossal, licking and sucking, and sucking and licking her way to that Caramel Crème she loved to taste.

"Oh baby! You breaking a brother off just right. Oh, damn. Well damn baby. Slow down ...a brother not trying to bust," Caramel Crème moaned.

"Oh yeah, well get ready cause Candy bout to ride Colossal into the sunset," she said.

"I got places to be. You know I need my prince."

"Oh, colossal is on his way," he belted.

Candy started getting ready for Colossal's entry. She grabbed colossal and wrapped her fingers around its monolithic girth. "Wow, you are big as a two liter."

"Oh Candy girl," said Caramel Crème.

Candy pulled Caramel Crème's pants all the way down and started an advance attack on colossal.

"Baby, wait, let me get a condom," said Shane.

"You don't need a condom."

Pulling away he declared, "No, we need a condom. I am getting married in a little over a month. You know the drill and what time it is!" said Caramel Crème.

"Look, let's do this. Nineteen minutes and your time will be up," said Candy.

Candy started slowly lowering her body onto Colossal, gliding it into her juicy wet pussy. As her pussy muscles loosened, Colossal entered with a gush and pushed straight up until he hit that G spot, like a marksman at target practice.

"Oh, damn. That's the shit baby. I love it when you hit this pussy right there," she moaned.

Caramel pushed Colossal deeper and deeper into Candy's pussy. Deeper and deeper Colossal's massive ten-inch girth knocked into the lips of Candy's pussy. Caramel felt the juices of Candy's pussy sliding down his inner thighs.

Smiling to himself, he pushed deeper and deeper.

"C'mon on baby, count with me," said Candy.

"Count? Did you say count with you?" asked a confused Caramel Crème.

Deeper and deeper, Colossal entered Candy's pussy. Deeper. Deeper. Colossal knocked into the lips of Candy's pussy. He stroked deeper and deeper.

"Come on baby, count with me," she repeated.

"What in the world? Count? Did you say count with you?" asked a still-confused Caramel Crème.

"Yep. Didn't you agree to twenty-five minutes in and out?" said Candy.

"Well I aim to please and meet your request. Fifteen minutes left. And you know I need to get all up in there."

"One-two. Oh-wee," she attempted.

"Not deep enough. I can still tell what you saying. Come on girl, ride this colossal dick. You're not riding him right. You still counting."

"Four –five-sixty two, one, -seven, nine Damn boy. Ooooooooooooh Colossal I want more," she continued in a state of bliss.

"Ummm, girl you know how to ride and make a brother feel good. Keep rolling them hips and milking Colossal. Ride this dick. Ummm girl!" he yelled. Caramel

Crème grabbed Candy's hips and pulled her down harder on Colossal. "Candy, girl ride this dick."

"Two, twenty-seven, eleven, tweeeeelve. Dam Car. .... you are grrrreat." She continued the quickie countdown.

"Go on girl. Milk Colossal and take all this cum in that juicy wet pussy. Ride it girl, ride this dick," he demanded. Caramel Crème tightened his hands on Candy's hips and busted a nut. Candy slid off his chest and off of Colossal.

At the same time, Caramel Crème rubbed Colossal, removing his condom.

"Time to go," said Candy.

"Damn baby I ain't even got my pants on yet. Can't a brother take a bath? You know I can't be smelling like sweet Candy when I get home."

Caramel crossed the room, went to the guest room, and started the shower. Water and steam quickly filled the space.

"Oh, hell no. Get out. Go home!" she demanded.

"Candy, girl you tripping. Baby look. I'm going to take a shower before I hit the door. Have fun with your friends." His comment was met with a resounding, "Oh hell no. My friends are waiting on me. Get out," said Candy.

"Don't be silly. I can't go home smelling like sweet candy. The candy is always sweet. But my woman won't be."

Pick up, Pick up, answer the phone. Her phone rang. "Look, that's my phone. You need to move. Can't you take a bath at home? After all, your woman is out with her moms."

"Candy, don't be silly. I love my woman," he confessed.

"Wow, how do you feel about me? You love your woman but Colossal loves me," she teased.

"I am not going to mess a damn thing up with my situation. What my future wife don't know won't hurt her!" he proclaimed, but he did not fool Candy.

"How you know? Maybe your future does know," she asked with a smirk.

"Awwright. Caramel Crème, wash Colossal in the sink and get out."

Come see bout me, I ate off the apple tree. Candy's phone rang again. Damn my phone is ringing again."

"Hello."

"Estimated time of arrival? I mean really bitch. ETA? We about to get on down Frenchmen without your late ass," the friendly voice asked.

"Girlie, I'm coming. Shannon, do not play with me. Would I ever miss a Thursday at Snug's? Look... getting dressed. Out the door in five minutes tops. Look, I see you in a few. Estimated time of arrival is fifteen minutes. Later Girlie. Bye." She said without emotion.

Driving toward her Thursday night outing, Candy's Mustang purred to life as she got on I-10 west. She checked the rearview mirror to make sure neither Caramel Crème nor his fiancé were following her. She thought aloud, "I'd had my fun, no a greeatt time with Colossal and now I want to have some more fun with the girlies." Her mind was on a bowl of gumbo and two for one Lemon drops. "Damn," she muttered, "I almost missed my Elysian Fields exit." To Candy, there was nothing like some good Nawlins' food and delicious drinks to complete an awesome Colossal experience and make it better.

"Smile girlie," she said to herself. "You already started your happy hour."

As she drove over the high-rise interstate and slowed at the 610 merge, her phone rang. Candy thought, *People, people, must we slow down here go straight or turn right? Just hurry up ... got places to be and people to see.*

Come see bout me I ate off the apple tree, her phone persisted.

"Yeah. What you want?" said a relaxed and annoyed Candy.

"ETA," said Shannon.

"Seven minutes over high- rise and approaching Elysian Fields. Later."

Candy approached the off ramp at Elysian Fields, merging left. She passed not one light, but two lights. She passed the park and thought, *Okay. Scan for a spot. Turning on Frenchmen. Wow. Move it, people. A spot just opened on the corner. Please nobody turn on Frenchmen ahead of me! No turn. No turn. No turn. Wow, it is a damn good night!* She daydreamed on her last sweet treat. "First a visit from Colossal, and now a parking spot on Frenchmen in front of Private Joy coffee shop."

Candy's phone continued to ring the popular second line song, *Come see bout me I ate off the apple tree.*

"ETA?" demanded the same voice.

"Shannon, if you don't stop ringing my phone off the damn hook." She barked. "I'm walking up Frenchmen now. Got a great spot in front of Private Joy," bragged Candy.

"Just wanted to tell your ass we are sitting in the window facing the street …didn't see you pass by," said Shannon.

"Cool."

"Girl did you stop and look at Private Joy's word of the day?" asked Shannon, knowing Candy's late ass probably did not notice. Shannon knew her friend well; she was only focused on two things, drinks, and men.

"No. What is it?" Candy inquired.

"Too cute. Gay. Gay means to feel happy, bright, carefree, and showy. Well that show does describe the strip on Frenchmen and its cast of regulars. You think Lillian's husband can say the same?" teased Shannon.

"Uhmmm Miss Messy, get off my damn line. I am walking through the door," exclaimed Candy. Buzz, Buzz, Buzz. Candy pulled her vibrating phone from her pocket and quickly read the text message. "Have fun with your girls but remember the real fun is always with us. Love you Crème."

Thursday

I n the café sat four girlfriends awaiting the fifth one's arrival. A frustrated Imani began asking questions. "Shannon, have you called Candy? Where is she? I hate this bullshit when we are all here on time and her ass makes us wait for her. She knows we meet here every Thursday. I'm going to tell Ms. Diva something this time. Every Thursday it's something new but it always means we have to wait on Candy."

"Look, Imani, I have called, and as usual I'm at the second line on the phone," explained Shannon.

"That girl and those damn brass band musical ring tones. Girl, Candy is show nuff a mess. How old are we? She still runs harder for the second line than she does for herself and her respect," said Imani.

A disbelieving Shannon snarled at Imani, "Imani stop it. You know you be running for the second line too." Imani couldn't help but laugh, this was quite true, she knew it, and so did all of New Orleans.

"True that," she happily replied. "I just handle my other business just as hard."

Imani gasped, "Lillian, is everything all right? We don't have a table and you done ordered yourself a drink?"

"Well today was crazy at school and I have had enough bull shit for one damn day," snapped Lillian, all the while thinking, she should have ordered something stronger. Imani nodded, winked at Joe, and ordered drinks for the gang.

"Greetings and Salutations girlies," sang Candy.

"Hey Candy. About time slow motion. Got damn … you crawled your way here?" The ladies all sang, sounding like a dazed flock of birds.

"What … y'all got jokes? Just needed to handle some last minute business for the hospital. Any w-h-o, it's crowed out on Frenchmen tonight. All the regulars are out and a few new faces too. Imani, pay attention, you might meet somebody worth going out with," she teased, unknowingly returning Imani's catty comments.

"Yeah right, Candy. Leave me alone. I'm just fine with my dating life," replied Imani.

Candy, who wasn't finished with her observations, asked, "What dating life?"

"I have a life and it's going just fine," Imani asserted, growing frustrated with Candy's comments.

In an effort to break up the argument, Lillian expressed herself.

"Ladies, you need to have a wonderful husband like me. Then you wouldn't need to be on a hunt every Thursday."

"Whatever," Lillian, grunted to the group.

Snug's was one of the best spots for great appetizers and killer drinks poured by Joe. Joe always outdid himself for Imani and the girlie's every Thursday night, and tonight was no different. Only one of the five was present and seated waiting for the others to show up for their set date. The five of them had met through school and work. College had been a great time, where the Thursday night meetings were born.

Imani slowly scanned the table, looking from left to right at her assembled friends, taking in every detail of the night. The ladies were sitting at their favorite window table—facing Frenchmen, looking out on the strip and all its travelers. Snug's was on the outer edge of the French Quarter, away from all the tourist traps. This strip was jazzy, busy, bright, but a little dim in spots. It was full of people walking with drinks in hand, doing their best. Imani thought, *I'm drunk, but that's my song stroll*, all the while stepping over stale piss and never missing a beat. The smell of good Creole food—the kind with plenty of the trinity (onion, bell pepper, and celery) and extra spice – mixed with trash while gas exhaust from passing cars, scented the air.

Alexis slowly waved her hand in front of Imani's face. "Earth to Imani. What are you thinking about?"

"Nothing. Well ladies what's happening?" said Imani.

Lillian rolled her eyes and opened her hands to wave over their present environment. "Why do we always come here? I mean every week we give the man our money... for what? Why can't we go to a nice African American bar and give us some play?" she declared as though making a political stand.

"Lillian, stop this shit. You drink more than the rest of us. What's up your ass tonight?" said Alexis.

"Nothing. I just feel as African American professional women we should give our businesses more play and respect. Why we got to come down here and support everybody but ourselves?" she asked.

"Attention, I have met the man of my dreams. I am leaving Schwegmann's grocery store for sure. Just as soon as he hooks me up with an allowance so I can leave the world of work behind me. Come on ladies y'all know the song, *No romance just some finance*. Got to have a j-o-b if you wanna get with me," said Shannon.

"Girl, I swear you are crazy," said Alexis.

Lillian sucked her teeth. "Okay Shannon who is it now?"

"The other day I saw Roxxy and she hooked me up. Every time I get my eyebrows done I meet a new man. I swear I owe my car, fur coat, a few trips, and too many privileges to count to Roxxy. She is the best brow specialist in the NOLA. Oh, the man's name is Derrick. Girl, I was at work, and you know how I do my patented *all you broke single girls need to adopt* basket check. I walk past the man wiggling my hips just a tad too much and smile," said Shannon.

"Girl, can you get to the point? Ain't nobody trying to hear your, Pussy can save the day stories. Some of us are married to wonderful men and enjoy that shit. I, myself, did not look for a brother to sponge off of and get rich. I looked for a man with intellectual thought and potential," said Lillian.

"Now where was I?" Shannon finished. "Oh yeah, I was walking and working my hips. I walk up, check for any sign of a woman, and swoop on in. Derrick was buying some fish and salad. So of course, that equals a health nut. Ladies, you need to adopt these rules of the game. You know my Moms got it on lock and she taught me what to do and how to work the pussy power since birth. So, I strolled over and said, 'Your wife must be so happy to come home to you.'"

"I was holding my breath with my fingers crossed," Shannon continued, "thinking, Oh my God. Please let him be single. I hate having to deal with wives. One, two, three. Come on God let him be single. A nice button down shirt, French cuffs, coral cuff links, nice slacks, clean crop cut. Smells nice, like FCUK out of French Connection. Anyway, we have been talking every day non-stop since meeting. We went for a run at Audubon Park. The man looks good, and didn't even break a sweat while we jogged. I am looking forward to making him sweat. We went for drinks at the Wine Loft, and Deanies' for some barbeque shrimp. We have been running and feasting all over town."

Imani looked over her assembled friends.

They all sat quietly, listening to Shannon go on and on about her new man and the Shannon System. Shannon was their colorful friend from Schwegmann's grocery store. Shannon was a pretty Creole girl the color of café au lait, with wavy hair, big brown eyes like silver dollars, and she was a perfect size ten. Shannon lived in the gym and on a diet. Her mom always told the girls, "You'll never be broke if you keep your figure tight, and smile bright, you'll have everything you can dream of ... suck a little dick you'll have more." Shannon practiced this motto daily.

"I'm loving how this brother gets down," said Shannon, breaking into Imani's thoughts.

"So what? You McDonald's now? You lovin it? I swear your ass needs to get a grip and start depending on yourself," said Lillian.

"I do depend on myself. I work every day. And pay bills with an options plan. I opt to pay with somebody else's money, but will pay with my own money if I have to. I will land a sponsor who treats me with material respect. A man displays his love by the quality of his gifts. I went to college and got a degree like the rest of you girlies. I just choose to use my pussy power to the best advantage," said Shannon.

An irritated Lillian inquired, "What the hell? Must it always be about sexing a brother and getting a gift?"

"Yes, Lillian it is always about getting a gift."

"What you getting from your husband?" asked Shannon.

Lillian was more than happy and eager to declare the goodness of her man.

"My husband is a wonderful man. He supports me in my career. He gave me a ring and a wedding in Armstrong Park. Don't you remember being there?"

"Yeah, girl I was there. But I'm also there when his raggedy ass is out and you are at home. You ever asked him where he is when we are in Snug's every Thursday?" Shannon smirked.

"No. My husband loves me and respects our marriage," said Lillian.

"Yeah, he respects your marriage," said Shannon.

"Stop it." Imani glared.

"Whatever, Imani," said Shannon.

Imani looked at Shannon and gave her the, Don't You Dare, look.

"Must you always try to keep the peace? Can't we have a little constructive conversation about the power of pussy and men and women?" said Shannon.

"Yes, we can. And I am looking forward to having a normal conversation about vaginas and men," said Imani.

"All right, what else is going on?" said Alexis.

Alexis turned her head and looked at Shannon over her shoulder. "I'm going to take your drink. Seriously, girl, every week we need to keep you off the sauce."

"What is it? Gang up on Shannon day?" Candy snapped.

"No. It's Thursday. Time for some jazz, good drinks, and appetizers. Look, this is our one night a week to kick it as a group and enjoy each other."

Alexis looked over the animated friends and asked, "Imani, how was your date last week?"

As Imani reminisced, she laughingly stated, "Well it was a date. Thank God it is over and everybody is still living."

"Come on girl, it was that bad?" asked Candy.

"No it was worse," blurted Imani.

"What happened this time? Where did you meet up?" asked a confused and amused Shannon.

Imani took a sip from her drink and began replaying the date.

"We went to the coffee shop on Westend," Imani said. "I sped from work, trying to beat the afternoon traffic traveling out of town. I made it to Starbucks with enough time to blot my face in the rest room while humming a tune or two. Applied some fresh Sugared Chicago

Chocolate lip-gloss. Y'all know I like nude makeup. While waiting, I finished reading a Brenda Jackson book for some inspiration. In her books no matter how fucked up the situation, the people always find a way to get it going and have some great sex. Moving it along, I figured a coffee shop on the lake at 5:30 pm would be a good spot to chat. It's spring, so there was a nice breeze off the lake. We sat outside watching the people go by. Girl, he was so, like beautiful and deep. I mean, I know I am a big girl. A card-carrying member of Weight Watchers for life … got to go walk or my ass will spread bigger than the Mississippi River and all that shit. But, he was nice, until his momma kept calling."

"Yeah, Yeah, Imani. What happened …is he hot or what? Did you sex him?" interjected Alexis.

"Did he get you a gift, or has he got gift giving potential?" asked Shannon.

"Did he talk about the future?" asked Lillian.

Imani just smiled at the friends and all the questions.

"Yes, Lillian he did mention the future. Shannon, he works as a Social Worker, so his resources would be limited as far as the gift giving you are used to. After all, we mental health people work hard for a little money. All while being expected to help the world," said Imani.

"Speak for yourself. I do quite well at Counseling Connections. I'm not looking for a man to save me. I'm looking for one to rendezvous around the world with. Nothing like salty sea air and penis to make a girlie feel good," said Alexis.

Candy jeered, "That's why you should have gone into management."

"Candy? Manager extraordinaire? No comment."

"Well, he was hot and taken," said Alexis.

"He is 6'2", single with no children, but unfortunately he is taken by his momma," Imani added. "He still is sucking his momma's tittie. Girl, if she didn't call thirty times in an hour. It was like she thought I was going to steal her son. His stats: single, no children, never been married, social worker. He has a little pouch. But at our age a little pouch is good."

"Girl. Men do not get pouches. They get beer guts," laughed Alexis.

"In that case he has a little beer pouch," Lillian laughed.

"Ha, Ha, Ha, let me finish." Imani continued. "The energy was great, music was playing. Then my song *Groove City* was playing and it kept me thinking about hand dancing. Being that it was 5:30, my mind was on food and points. I swear my mind picks the weirdest times to focus in on hunger and a desire to eat everything. It smelled like I was sitting in Acme Oyster House down the street. The grill and the smell of fresh seafood was everywhere. Anyway, we talked about trips and traveling and future plans. Girls, the man is so fine ... with heavenly smooth chocolate skin. His teeth look white, like pretty snowflakes on TV." She thought a moment, and then declared, "I had passion fruit lemonade. We chatted about the city. His momma called. We chatted about the conference and being in Miami for a fun filled week of beach and mental health. His momma called. Imagine my amazement at meeting a man from NOLA in Miami. His momma called. Girl, we were deep into dancing at Mangoes' when his momma called again. I swear she's riding a brother's dick so hard she will never have grand children because she won't give a girl a chance to take a ride." As Imani told her story of the beautiful suitor and his co-dependent mother, the group shared in her disgust.

It was a typical night at Snug's. The Marsalis brothers took the stage and everyone started mingling and dancing. The group spotted and designated an unsuspecting gentleman as an outstanding man and sent him a drink. To date only five men had inspired such an occasion. But, they were always looking to add to their number.

Michael walked in with his smooth, walk on water self, and Candy thought, *Nothing like a good-looking fine ass man to make you want to forget all the shit you mama told you not to do.* He inspired everybody to momentarily adopt Shannon's philosophy. He was the first male to inspire them to break into song, "Outstanding......boy, you are outstanding, boy you knock me out."

Michael was Hershey, with skin as smooth as chocolate pudding, pearly white teeth, and broad shoulders. He made women say hello to the penis without hearing a word he had to say.

"What up ladies?" Michael flirted.

Everyone turned and smiled as Michael joined the approaching trio of fellas who strolled toward the ladies' table.

Anthony said, "Why you got that mean mug, Lillian?"

Lillian said, "Shannon is telling us all about her new man and how wonderful he is. Her brand new

Mr. Perfect. You know her new money, sex, gym, and everything else in between. Just don't get married cause that's when they show their asses and true selves."

Anthony started to laugh, and then signaled the waitress to bring another round of drinks.

"Hey man, I think I just found my wife. Just check out the chick at the bar.

Anthony and Rashaad just shook their heads and laughed at Corey.

Alexis stated, "Damn negro, what is your problem? You know you and Shannon need to hook up. Every week it's another Mr. /Mrs. Wonderful. When y'all going to find yourselves?"

Corey said, "I just found myself at the bar."

Tap. Tap. Tap. Imani tapped her empty glass to the beat, signaling the friends to stop. "Let us pray for peace, new drinks, and another Thursday to see Joe!"

Corey laughed and turned and walked over to the girl at the bar. He was sporting a neat faded haircut and linen slacks with a burnt orange shirt. Corey was a big man who moved like a shadow. He always appeared out of nowhere to be right in the center of things.

The group always wondered how he did it. Alexis loved to call him Mr. Magic. The last two gentlemen of the group were vastly different from the first. Anthony and Rashaad could be brothers, based on their attitudes and physical appearances. Both were six feet plus, clean cut, well-groomed, manicured and pedicured, dressed from the pages of GQ.

These groups of friends greatly complimented each other.

"Well girlies and gentlemen I am about to roll out," said Joe, the group's private bartender, or so he made them feel.

"Thank you, Joe," said Imani. "You are my blond lover. My one and only true blond love. You love to hook a sister up with the best spirits in town. I love you for hooking me up."

"See you next week sweetie," said Joe.

"Thank you Joe," the girls said in chorus. Another good night at Snug's.

Imani

mani strolled to her car after saying bye to the gang. She quietly thought about how she would deal with going to work and dealing with people without Thursday nights on the strip.

Another Thursday at Snug's -- it was good to see the friends, talk shit, and look for a potential man, Imani thought. *Every Thursday, I dance, mingle, and introduce myself to three new men. It is practice for me to come early to the strip and hit another bar before going to Snug's and meeting my friends.*

Alone and at her house, heels, jeans, shirt, bra all hit the floor at the closing of the door. Imani's house was a super sexy sparsely furnished space with contemporary furniture. A sofa, two cube tables—one for books, pictures, and African art; the other for a TV and DVD player, a pub and a contemporary bedroom set completed the furniture in her house. The bed set and room were covered in lavender because purple was her favorite color. Imani started her nightly rituals to journal, meditate, and exercise, creating a peaceful space. Imani started journaling, focusing on her own personal problems:

How am I going to reach my goals? All day long I help other people solve their own problems, listen to their shit, and work to enlighten others. But for me, I am unable to move forward, lose weight, or a find a friend. It seems every man I meet is unavailable, or in-love with their mommas--bringing brand new meaning to baby momma drama. Every day, I ask clients what are three things they are doing to move towards a goal? What is my goal? My goal has been to drop a few pounds and run the streets. Now I don't know what my goal should be. One- go out, two- walk with an exercise tape, three- ... damn ... no three. All right journal, tomorrow I will catch a cardio class at X-Your Size Inc. uptown and try to find a third thing for me to do.

Imani paused from journaling to answer the phone. Damn, it was Lillian calling to fuss about her husband. Imani and Lillian talked at least twice a week about Lillian's relationship. They had hung out for years, since grade school.

Lillian had arrived at home to find a note and no husband. He had dropped the kids off at her mother's house and gone out with the boys -- i.e., his other woman. Lillian cried at least once a week about her husband, her marriage, and her job. Her life was focused on how everybody else was fucking up, but not on what she was doing.

Now, Imani asked, "What's up?" *We just left Snug Harbor. How could anything be wrong?*

Lillian slowly exhaled and started fussing. "Damn he took the kids to Mom, and then went out with that woman. He always puts her first. He never takes me out, but every chance he gets, he's out with his friends. When his friends call, looking for him, he is already supposedly out with them. When I ask him about it, he just says he was running late and he met up with them after they called. Every week he parades his whore all over town … like I'm not here, plus, his Mom and family cover for his raggedy ass. Always saying he is over there visiting with them, knowing damn well he's not there."

"Lillian what do you want?" Imani asked. "Have you asked yourself what you really want? Could you please do that? Pause, look in the mirror, and think about who you are. Girl, hold your breath and think about who you are. One. Two. Three."

"Imani, I have what I want. A husband, two beautiful kids, and a house uptown on a street lined with fruit trees."

"All right, Lillian, so why are you calling me, if you have what you want?"

"I want a husband and a man for myself. I want a partner in life. I want a friend," Lillian said.

Imani closed her journal and put down her pen. She began rolling her shoulders back while making circles with her head to relieve the building stress. Imani started, "Lillian what have you done?"

What do you mean, what have I done? I work, clean house, run all over town taking lessons, and try to be a good wife. I work even when my husband does not. I never complain about his shit and don't confront him about his woman. I just hope he doesn't make a baby in the street. I should have my husband's only children."

"Okay, Lillian I understand you work hard with the kids. But have you told your husband how you truly feel? Have you demanded he go to counseling or even demanded he leave his woman alone?"

"I know I need to do something," Lillian agreed. "But, I don't want him to leave me. I want my kids to have a real Dad and a family life. I grew up without a Dad, feeling alone and isolated. I always wanted someone to protect me. My Mom would say, "Don't be like me … get married, have a partner, because raising kids is hard work." Why can't he ever stay home with the kids? It's like we dance around each other on an inflated balloon, too afraid the air will ooze out and cause us to fall. I just want to stay on the balloon with my kids and my husband. I want a marriage. I want a faithful, loving husband, and father for my children. My girls will not grow up like me …with a mother daydreaming on a man that did not marry her, my Dad, and focused on her husband that died young. She never recovered or let me forget."

Attempting to not sound anxious and insensitive, a supportive Imani responded, "Well, Lillian. It sounds like you have accepted the situation, so why are you whining about him?"

"I swear I don't know why I call your ass. You just don't get it, Imani. You don't want a man or a family. But, if you ever get one you will understand. You'll see why I'm always so sad."

"All right Lillian. I just hope you can find the balloon big enough to hold you and your husband up."

Shannon

New Orleans East. Shannon dragged out of Schwegmann's grocery store feeling exhausted. It was the seventh of the month. Everybody had money by the seventh from child support to food stamps for seniors. They all had money and were pushing through the grocery store, buying goods and throwing things around, changing choices and putting stuff everywhere but where it belonged. All this money equaled hard long days at Schwegmann's for Shannon.

It had been a week since she met Derrick at the store. The past week had been filled with dinners, shopping, runs in Audubon Park, and late night chats. Shannon was truly enjoying this man.

Shannon picked up her cell phone and quickly dialed Derrick's number.

"What's up?" he asked.

"Just leaving work. Can we go out tonight? I am super tired from work and everybody running thru the grocery store at the same minute," Shannon replied.

Derrick slowed down, so he would miss the down elevator with his co-workers as they left the building.

"Sure Shannon," he told her. "We can go out, but can we take a ride? I feel like going to the casino in Biloxi."

"Derrick, that's an hour's drive and I'm hungry, tired, and not feeling like waiting that long. I just want to spend some time with you."

"Well that's what I plan on doing. You can come or not. But, what happened to the girl with all the energy, who wanted to keep me happy and pleased. What ... you don't have time for me? You met somebody else at Schwegmann's? You been talking to your dumb ass, no having men girlfriends? They been filling your head about all this stuff. You don't want to take a ride. Fine. I'll call somebody else. She will be more than happy sitting in the co-pilot's seat in my Benz. You decide." Click.

I can't believe he just hung up on me. Negro thinks a couple of dinners entitle him to what? I'm going to call his ass back. Who does he think he's talking to?

Shannon hit re-dial on the phone, pressing 504-223-5467.

"Derrick."

"What!" he roared.

"Are you having a bad day or what? I can't believe that's how you're going to speak to me. What is your problem? How you going to threaten me with some chick? Like I'm worried about another female. Did you forget you are attempting to take me out? Don't you want to spend some time with me?"

"Yeah! I am tired but I do want to spend time with my girl after work."

"Okay. Derrick. I hear you."

"Look. I told you what I want to do; now you need to be ready when I knock or just don't call me back any more."

"Okay, Derrick I'll be ready when you get here but your ass needs to bring it down a notch or two and remember who you are dealing with."

Shannon slammed the phone down. *This Negro must be losing his mind. How's he going to talk to me with that tone? He must have forgotten about the power of pussy. He ain't got and he won't get none at the rate he is going... that Negro must be crazy. He will not talk to me like that. The nerve of him putting bass in his voice. Coming at me like I'm desperate to be with his ass. I have choices; after all, tonight I will be seeing him while looking for a new friend. A girl has to have a man to get her next man. Nobody wants someone that nobody else wants ... besides a few tricks and I bet I could get that hot Chloe bag in Saks. I've been checking that out for a minute ... a few tricks equals a good old fashioned shop til you drop explosion.*

Shannon dragged herself into her apartment and slipped out of her work clothes. She began to get ready for her date. She stopped the tub and allowed the lavender vanilla bubble bath to fill up the tub and scent the entire apartment. She thought, *Nothing like a cup of tea and some lavender to relieve some stress. I got to get something out the deal soon or I must be slipping. Damn, this water is too hot, I guess I will call Imani while it cools a bit. Talking to Imani always puts a smile on my face, as she never has a man. I can always wow her with my men stories, and frequent gifts. She is sweet, green, and always has sugar in her voice, as well as good intentions. She is the kind of friend everyone enjoys but can't seem to figure out. Imani can always put a smile on my face.*

"Hey girl what you doing?" said Shannon.

"Just got in from a cardio class at X Your Size Gym uptown. The fitness instructor must have dementia ...

that lady can never get the count or get the numbers together. Five more, then you get to five, and she is saying two, just three more to go. I'm thinking about a slice of cake from Royal Cakery. Cake there is so good, I swear it's better than sex and chocolate. Every girl knows few things are better than sex and chocolate. I want a slice of white cake with strawberry filling, a glass of Zinfandel, or maybe some Champagne punch, maybe a white wine spritzer. I don't know. I just want something good," said Imani.

Shannon was not trying to hear about cake. Abruptly she interrupted Imani. "Imani, Imani, Imani. Can you stop and focus? Must everything be about food, liquor, or liquor and food? Slow down. How are you going to get a man if you are always focused on eating and drinking? Anyway, my new man wants to go to Biloxi but I told him it's the middle of the week and I'm tired. I have to go to work in the morning. If I miss work, he must be ready to take over all my bills, or a few bills. Girl ain't nothing like having a man to pay your bills and a free check to play with. Can I put you on speaker while I bathe?"

"Shannon, why are you going to Biloxi if you're tired? Don't you have to work tomorrow?" retorted Imani.

"Why else, Imani? You tell me. To get to all the good stuff. He drives a beautiful fully loaded Blue Benz, works downtown, has no kids. He is the ultimate party with a purpose guy. My purpose is having fun and getting paid for it," said a boastful Shannon.

"What to wear? Girlie, remember our last trip to the mall ... what should I wear?"

"I don't know. Don't you have outfits planned for the ultimate seduction?" Imani said.

"Well true," Shannon replied. "I just finished pulling out clothes and trying to figure out the perfect simple chic outfit. I want to look like I didn't try hard, while still working it. Let me see. Got it."

"Got what?" asked a puzzled Imani.

"I will wear a goddess dress in royal blue, multi-color print with a solid blue belt. Some black Kenneth Cole split toe cork heel ankle strap sandals. Look Imani, I need to go and finish getting beautiful. Bye Girlie hopefully you will have a date soon."

Shannon began her assessment of progress, a sort of beauty checklist. Hair and makeup. Check. Perfume strategically placed to solicit unwavering desire. Check. Lotion slathered all over. Check. *Girlie you are looking good. Just look at your self in the wall size mirror. As my girlie Candy would say, "Mirror, Mirror on the wall who's the sexiest of all?" Yep mirror, you are lucky to just get a peep at me.*

Bam, Bam, Bam. Flowers … a beautiful arrangement of daisies …filled the peephole. Shannon opened the door to Derrick, who was carrying the flowers. As she glanced at him, she couldn't help but think,*"Oh, God, thank you for blessing me with a man so fine and wealthy. Square toe Ferragamo espresso brown shoes, Theory slacks, Robert Gram button down French cuff shirt. Thank you, Lawd. A man who constantly dresses well and looks like he belongs to step in line with me. But …this Negro better get his attitude together 'cause men don't talk to me any kind of way. After all, I'm the perfect woman; cute, sexy, not an ounce of fat, and hazel brown eyes. He better recognize the gift of my presence."*

"Derrick, let me get my purse and we can go," she greeted.

"Hurry up, woman. I would like to eat today," the rough voice admonished.

Shannon winced, "Hey, let go of my arm."

"Well hurry up then. Move it! Move it!"

He did speak as though talking to an animal. "Derrick, slow the fuck down. Biloxi and Beau Rivage ain't going anywhere," she yelled.

"Let's go woman," he demanded.

"Is this how you treat your patients at the hospital?" she asked.

"No but this is not where I earn my money," Derrick sneered.

Candy

S nug's with girlies, fun, and an awe-inspiring night.
"All right, madam. You didn't want one of us to
walk you to your car," Corey said to Candy.

"No just thinking. Hadn't really thought about it.
Anyway, I'm right here in front of Private Joy's coffee
shop. Did you look in the window at the word of the
week?"

"Na, Candy I hadn't looked, but it must be great."

"Thanks, Corey. See you next week."

As she left Corey, Candy thought, *"Time to do a little
research. Once again I am on my nightly cruise to check out
Justin's house."*

Justin served as Candy's boo, while Shane a.k.a
Caramel Crème was her ultimate obsession. She continued her inquisition. *How is my companion not trying
to be companion-like anymore? Why has he stopped calling?
Why no texts? He doesn't even look at me at the hospital?
Wonder what he has heard? Does he know about Shane?
Well Caramel Crème is my delicious treat. All men adore
me. I am always the center of attention. He is going to tell me
what's up with this.*

Candy entered the car, adjusted the air, and turned the radio on full blast. She knew she would arrive at Justin's in ten minutes. She made a left onto Elysian Fields. She drove, one light, two lights, three lights. As she turned right at St. Claude, she turned the lights off. She said to herself, "Pay attention girlie we need a good parking spot. Every spot is taken. Why must he live in Bywater? Every spot within a damn block is taken." Normally around the corner, there was a good spot. She took her heels off and put her tennis on with gloves, and said, "Lawd have mercy. Nobody can see me like this. Tennis shoes with my dress. Damn. What you looking at? Acting like you never seen a woman with a dress and tennis!" she admonished a passerby.

"Hurry up, hurry up" she whispered. She started to Justin's house with a nice easy pace. Candy did not want to attract too much attention. In an ongoing conflict with her conscience she thought, *Damn, I should have borrowed a dog to make it look more natural. Why are the blinds down? I know he has a woman in there with him.* The sound of the music was everywhere. In a state of paranoia, she continued to rant her beliefs that he had someone in his house. She knew he was not trying to play, Candy girl. She had already established in her mind that she would bust his ass and he would not feel the end of it. She was going make his life a living hell at the hospital. How was he going to try and play her? She was convinced that she just needed to get a little bit higher to see into that top window. She stepped onto the garbage can, and thought, *Damn, I can't see the living room. Music? What is he doing? I thought he was busy working another shift, like he told me. I call, he lies. Nobody plays Candy.* As she got down from the garbage can, she decided to go next door. She carefully checked for bystanders, looking left, then right, no one was out. *Pick up, Pick up, answer the phone,* her phone rang. Anxiously she thought, *Not now.* She pressed reject.

She continued her 'bout business' walk down the alley until she reached the fence. With Foxy Brown precision, she quickly scaled the fence, moving the lawn chair so that it stood in the way of an ill-fated Justin. As Candy stepped up to the window she peered in, but the anxiety only intensified as she strained to find him. Where was he? Why couldn't she see him? She could hear his music. "Look, he is by himself. Snap, get down before he sees you."

She now admonished herself.

Candy was making her way to the car when the phone started again. *Pick up, Pick up, answer the phone,* it blared. Sitting in her ride, she changed her shoes. She wondered what had happened, but he was alone.

"Yeah. Where are you?" asked the voice at the other end of the line.

"In the car. What is it? Pick on Candy day? I was a few minutes late and everybody got a crawfish up their ass. Be easy and chill," she snapped.

"Call me when you get home?" said the voice.

Candy agreed, "Ah right, Bye." Candy continued playing with the phone to read Caramel Crème's newest text massage. "Got your panties."

After having humiliated herself over an ill attempt at stalking Justin, Candy returned home in a state of confusion. She just needed a good long bubble bath with a drink to calm her nerves, then she would return Shannon's call.

"Hey! Shannon girl what's up? We just left Snug's ... what you need."

"You were in such a hurry. Where you off to?" questioned Shannon.

In an unconvincing tone, she responded, "Nowhere, just home."

"Right, funny girlie. If home was the answer you would have been chatting earlier when I called," teased Shannon.

"Anyway ... what?" Candy interrupted.

Laughing and convincing to no one but herself, Shannon replied, "What? What I just called. How's that doctor from the hospital?"

"He is good ... just worked an extra shift today."

"Candy, you would tell me if something was up?"

In an effort to deter her friend from pursuing the investigation any further, Candy retorted, "Shannon, nothing is up, just wanted to ride in my car and think about what's next. Can't a girl have a peaceful moment?"

Alexis

"Hey Suga!" Alexis kissed Michael on the cheek. "What you doing out here?"

"Just waiting on you to open up," he flirted.

"You know I'm just getting in from Snug's and out of the tub. Nothing like a rain bath soak to relax away all your stress. Come on in Suga, I was just about to start your dinner."

"I like when all the stress is gone. Baby, you don't have to fix me a meal.

How the girlies doing?" Michael asked.

"Everybody is awright. Nothing much new. Shannon got a new man, Lillian mad at her man, Imani had a crazy ass date, and come to think of it, Candy didn't mention a man at all this week. Did you eat?"

Alexis rambled off her girlfriends' gossip as if it was the mid-day soap recap. "Well, maybe she got somebody."

"No, I didn't eat. I'd much rather nibble on you and eat one of your protein bars later." His flirts persisted.

"I don't think so, no man for Candy and no protein for you. She just didn't mention nobody. So that's what's been happening with my bars. What you doing eating protein? Please tell me you are not trying to do anything to my body over there. I enjoy every inch of you tooo damn much for you to be making changes with protein." Now she was flirting.

She entered the kitchen, switched on a light, and put a saucepan on the stove. As she looked inside the refrigerator, she offered, "I have some salmon and tilapia. Which one sweetie?"

"Already told you a protein bar later will do just fine with me." Michael pulled Alexis into his arms from behind and began kissing her on the neck. "I told you, I don't want dinner, I want you. You just took a bath. You don't need to be cooking for me."

"Salmon or Tilapia? Stop. You need to eat. I been with you long enough to know you haven't eaten since early this morning," she stated while savoring his lips on her flesh.

"No baby, I haven't eaten but a nibble here and there will be good," asserted Michael.

"Fish?" Alexis asked.

"Salmon if you insist," Michael answered.

"Yes, I insist and I insist later you nibble away. Suga, open the wine." she replied.

Michael walked over to the fridge got a bottle of wine and uncorked it. "A glass for the cook and one for me."

"Thank you Suga."

"Let me plate you some salad. What kind of dressing you want?" said Alexis.

"Vidalia Onion," replied Suga. "Salmon three minutes on one side. We have three more minutes before the fish is ready. What can we do?" she taunted.

"We can kiss and kiss some more."

"Boy, come on, you need to stop. Last time we wound up burning the fish,"

Alexis reminisced on the smoking hot evening.

"That's why I said you don't need to feed me," he laughed.

Michael leaned over and pressed Alexis against the fridge. "A little wine for you and another sip for me. I like your nightshirt."

As much as she did not want to give in, her blushing response was, "You like my shirt?"

"Yep. It has the right amount of breast exposure." Michael was now turning up the heat.

"Come on baby, stop it. Your fish is going to burn. I want to take care of you in every way."

Alexis plated the salmon and created a place for Michael to eat. "Come on baby sit down and enjoy."

"Baby, come here," he begged once more.

"What, Mike? I'm going get things together in the bedroom. Got a few candles to light. I need to pick up from earlier. I was running out the door to meet the girlies and didn't pick up. I would like to invite my man to a clean space. Now eat, so you can come nibble. You did say you were looking to nibble away."

"Yeah I'm looking to nibble. Baby this salmon is delicious. What's this sauce?"

"Nothing Suga, just a little love for my outstanding man," Alexis boasted.

Michael finished eating, rinsed his plate, washed his hands, and headed for the bedroom. Michael's eyes followed Alexis' movement around her room. The candle light and rain bath scent started another round of outstanding movement between them.

Alexis stopped hanging up clothes upon seeing Michael in the doorway.

"Where were we in the kitchen? I recall we were kissing up against the refrigerator and getting ready for this right here," Michael said.

"Suga. Come lay with me."

Michael slowly took off his clothes. He put his shoes in the closet, followed by slacks on a hanger beside a Robert Gram, French cuff, cream-colored shirt; cuff links on the dressing table with keys and glasses. Michael walked to the closet and closed the door.

Alexis watched Michael's every movement while caressing her breast through her nightshirt. Sucking in her breath and closing her eyes Alexis patiently waited for Michael to come over to the bed.

"Come here baby," she beckoned.

Michael went to the bathroom and washed his face.

"Come here baby, I'm ready," she assured him.

Michael smiled to himself and thought of how good this woman really was. "Yeah baby, I'm ready too."

Sucking Michael's fingers was only the beginning. Touching her navel before slowly caressing her couchie hair, then spreading her legs open to nibble on his personal treat, Michael enjoyed being Alexis' Suga.

They moaned together as he enjoyed being her Suga and she enjoyed being his baby. Alexis closed her eyes, counted, and thought, *Thank you Jesus! I got me a man now. Please Suga don't mess up... you are one of my greatest blessings. A fine ass man with a job and style. Lawd have mercy! I may have to stay at the grocery store making sure you never need to go anywhere but here and home. Oh, my God…I got a man that showers me with gifts and respect. Girl, you got it together, he loves you. Can you love him back? He displays love all the time.*

A firm hand came over her and grabbed her hips and pulled her forward. Michael loved for Alexis to ride almost to the end, and then he would flip her on her back.

"Oh Baby….. I love you so much," he said, wrapping his arms around Alexis like a Snuggie blanket.

"Suga, Suga, Suga, I need to breathe," she pleaded.

"What baby… I love you soo much. Oh, girl a brother about to bust. Damn baby….. Ow weee. Girl you the bomb," Michael declared.

"Baby unwrap me. You sho nuff the shit. Mike. Mike. Let a sister breathe."

He laughed, "Okay baby we cool. I'm moving."

"Thank you Suga."

Alexis kissed Mike on the chest, both cheeks, forehead, and finally on his lips. "I love you Suga. Job well done baby. Our last trip was the bomb. I enjoyed spending a lovely weekend exploring the magnificent mile in Chicago. Suga what's my surprise?" she asked anxiously.

"What surprise?"

"You are so good to me. Every few weeks we get away and play like lovers. Just thought maybe because I did such a good job cooking tonight, you might give your baby a hint."

Michael got up, went to the bathroom, washed his hands, and filled the tub with water. Baby got a hint. Come get in the tub with me."

Lillian

Driving home from her mother's house, Lillian contemplated her life and her marriage to Jared. "Girls please be quiet," she said. "Mommie is trying to get us home without running off the road. Did you guys do anything with Daddy before he dropped you off at Gram's?"

"We had McDonald's with Dad before going by Grams."

McDonald's? This Negro fed my babies McDonald's. He won't eat no damn McDonald's but he will feed our babies some damn McD's.

Lillian pulled into the gate.

"Get out little ladies. We need to get inside and ready for school in the morning. Momma needs to get you inside and call Auntie Imani."

"Hey girl, what are you doing? I know we just left Snug's but I'm too damn mad. This Negro left the girls with Mom to go out with the fellas again. I only ask for one night a week, and Jared brings them to Mom to go out with the fellas," said Lillian. "Yeah I hear you with your smart ass. And yes my balloon is big enough for me, my husband, my girls, and got damn Big Bird, heffa," replied Lillian.

"Little ladies come to the back. Time to start getting ready for bed and school."

"Mom, is Daddy going to be here to read us a story?" said the girls.

"Baby, Momma don't know but, don't worry, I will read you guys a story."

Lillian added honey to her first cup of Oolong tea, hoping it would bring her some peace and some sleep. It was nice enough hanging with the girlies, but did Imani need to be so damn blunt and perfect? If she had a man, she wouldn't be able to act all fucking peaceful.

Another cup a tea and little more honey, just as Jared walked in.

"Hello where did you go, Jared?"

"Out," said Jared.

"Would it kill you to stay home with the girls one night per week?" said Lillian.

"I did stay home with the girls. Drink your tea and leave me alone."

"What? Do you hear me talking to you?"

"Yeah, I hear you and I'm finished," said Jared. He walked into the girls' bedroom and kissed them good-night before going to his own room. Hanging up jeans and a Polo shirt, he returned the Timberlands to the closet before taking his cell phone into the shower.

Bam, Bam, Bam. "Negro where have you been?" said Lillian.

"Look, Lillian I answered all I was going too when I walked through the door. Now you need to sit down and leave me alone. Can't a brother go out, grab a drink, without all the damn nagging? I mean really, you make me sick with the fifty questions," said Jared.

"Well, if I didn't have to worry that our girls and me might walk up on you and one of your women then, I wouldn't ask so many questions," said Lillian.

"Look I'm taking a shower and going to bed. I already told you the truth.

Goodnight. Anyway, I wasn't …and do not go …out with other women."

"Goodnight again," said Lillian.

Okay, Jesus. I love this man, but he worries me every day. I've caught him more than once with somebody. Both of us walked away like we didn't see each other. But, I know he looked me dead in the eye before gently kissing his woman on the check. I saw him drag his fingers all over her face. Gently like a feather touching a baby's bottom. I love our life. Jared is a beautiful man, kind, sexy, and sweeter than sweet. I love our house in uptown, New Orleans, our girls, everything. Why can't he stay home, damn it? I want a husband. I want to be a wife. I want to be a married woman with a wonderful husband. I need you to fix this and us. I love him!

"Good morning, Trenell. How are things at Counseling Connections this morning?" said Imani.

"Well, Alexis is in a session this morning. The interns are not in yet. Shannon called ... sounds like she is in a crisis. Told her you were not here and Alexis was in session. Imani, we have a problem. There is a potential client who's been calling all day long. Its 9:30 and she has already called seven times trying to get a canceled appointment. She called yesterday with great attitude. She was referred via Coco down at Chocolates. You might want to explain Professional Counseling services to Coco. After all, this is a business. Our clients won't be able to get through at the rate she calls."

"One thing at a time, Trenell, I will contact the client and have Alexis call Coco," Imani assured her.

Trenell quickly remembered, "Oh, she has a consult scheduled Monday. I explained to her impatient gotta be seen today, crying, and screaming in the phone self that you just can't walk up in here and see somebody. The counselors have schedules and clients."

"Trenell, this is a business, but our mission is to help others. I will call this woman. Did you give her crisis info?" said a concerned Imani.

Blowing her off with a few hand waves, she replied, "Yeah, yeah, Imani, I know the rules. We like our bonuses around here. Ain't nobody trying to let us get sued. I'm trying to go on vacation with my friends to Viva Las Vegas."

"What's that number?" asked Imani.

"The sticky on your desk," said Trenell.

Imani ended the conversation with a breathy, "As always thank you in advance."

Upon entering her office, Imani gave a brief inspection of the room, noticing the sticky note. Immediately she placed her briefcase in the client seat and headed to the phone. "Good morning, May I speak with Shay Waters?"

"Speaking," said Shay.

"Well, this is Imani Flowers calling from Counseling Connections. I understand you have an appointment for a consultation on Monday."

"Yes, I need you to fix everything. I married the man of my dreams. Everything was perfect. But, now he won't do anything for me and or with me," said Shay.

"Hello, Hello. I need you to stop talking now. I am a Professional Counselor. We do not counsel on the phone. I just wanted to call and confirm your appointment and receipt of crisis information. Do you have numbers to call in case of an emergency?" said Imani.

"Yes," replied Shay.

Imani continued to ensure that proper procedures were followed. "Did the receptionist explain the consultation process?" she asked.

"Yeah, she said I couldn't come in until Monday at four. That is entirely too long to wait. I need to be back on schedule," whined the anxious caller.

Shay's anxiety was met with an assertive, "Shay, did you hear me earlier?" from Imani.

"Yeah I heard you," she complained.

"Well someone from the staff will meet with you on Monday. That person will explain the counseling process, our services, and the groups that are offered. We look forward to helping you with your mental health needs. We will contact you if a cancelation occurs," closed Imani. Imani was used to anxious clients and it was simply too early to fret over one. She decided instead to visit Alexis.

On her way to see Alexis in her office, she reminisced about their first meeting.

Alexis and I met and became fast friends while I was in school studying to become a counselor. Her motto was to call folk on their shit and that if you don't call their bluff they would never grow. "Good morning, Alexis. How are you?" asked Imani.

"Girl, I'm good, have thirty minutes before my next session," replied Alexis.

"Well, aren't we lucky? I have back to back sessions," Imani said.

"Oh hell no. It's Friday. You need to stop listening to all them problems on Friday," said Alexis.

"Alexis, stop it."

"Stop nothing," declared Alexis. "Everybody needs a break."

Imani thought Alexis' statement was true but a little unprofessional. "Well, this is a practice and a business.

Look, I'm going back to my office and get ready for my next client," she answered.

"Ah right Ms. Counselor Supreme. Remember, it's Friday. You need to go out and have some fun," Alexis declared in a taunting and authorative tone.

"Alexis, did you forget about last night? We all just met and went to Snug's."

"No, I didn't forget. You need to go out and find somebody to have fun with," said Alexis.

"Okay friend. Right after you meet and start running behind a man all day," said Imani.

Caramelized Crème Candy

"How my sweet Candy doing today?"

"I'm good Shane. What brings you here today?" said Candy.

"Candy why you tripping all of a sudden? We have been kicking it for the last fifteen months without any problems," Shane snapped.

He knew the rules but was acting like they were a couple, where, he has, privileges.

"Candy it's Friday. Last night I passed back by your house, thinking you would be back from Snug's, but you weren't here. Where did you go?" said Caramel Crème.

Quickly she thought and replied, "I know your ass ain't asking questions like we are a couple. Look. I needed to clear my head, so I went for a ride in my car."

"Candy it's dangerous for you to be riding around all night."

"Look, Caramel Crème, it wasn't all night but what do you care anyway?" said an annoyed Candy.

"Well, look …I see you are cruising for us to fight all night. We don't fight, Candy. What's wrong?"

"Nothing," said Candy.

"Nothing. You act like something is very wrong."

"Like I said …nothing. What brings you here?" replied Candy.

"I enjoyed getting with you yesterday before you went to Snug's. I wanted to finish what we started," said Caramel Crème in a boastful manner.

"What? Where is your wifey?" she asked.

"Candy, stop trying to pick a fight and come here. Wrap your arms around me and invite me inside."

"Inside?" She tried to stay firm but was quickly caving in.

"Yes inside your apartment and inside my candy treat. Baby I love you," said Caramel Crème.

"I love you too." *Damn. Just look at his ass. Why must he smell, and look so damn good. Lawd knows he is perfect for me. Just gotta keep working this man so he knows he is perfect in me and with me.* "All right my crème come in."

"What's for dinner Candy?" he asked.

"Oh, I made some Curry Tofu with spicy stir-fry veggies, spinach with green and yellow mango salad with fish oil and ginger dressing. To wash it all down, some ginger mango tea. Dinner is the perfect combination of sweet and spicy -- like me. Will you being staying for dinner?" said Candy,

"Yeah, Candy I want to stay for dinner and just hang out with you all night."

"Okay my Caramel Crème, set the table, and once dinner is over you can serve up some delicious Caramel Crème mousse. You know Colossal and me are best friends. Too bad you are trying to ruin our wonderful friendship," she teased.

"Candy you need to stop with the smart ass comments." His tone was serious.

She met his tone with an even more serious dialogue. "My comments are not smart." She thought, *If only you knew how smart I am. You think you can lay up and sex me and go home to your pretty fiancé. I think not. Candy gets what Candy wants. Right now, I want Caramel Crème and a little crème in my life forever. I will have you.* "Caramel I'm going use the bathroom. Keep an eye on our dinner sweetie."

"Sure. Nobody wants burned tofu. What in the world does that taste like? Candy next time we are going to have real food."

"We are having real food," said Candy. Candy entered her bathroom and left Caramel Crème in the living room. While in there she removed her makeup and rid herself of the tell tale working woman signs and donned the dress of Aphrodite and the sweet aroma of the goddess herself.

Candy returned from the bathroom to notice Caramel Crème wearing jeans, a Got Crabs tee shirt, and tennis. "Did you go to work today?" Candy asked.

"Of course I went to work; I just wanted to spend the rest of my day relaxing with you."

"So that's what we call it now?" said Candy.

"Look, Candy stop that," he demanded.

Candy looked clean and crisp. Her face was free of makeup and she was wearing a multi-color bold flower print maxi dress, and tan split toe sandals. Her hair was pulled back in a high ponytail at the top of her head. Upon her return, she realized Caramel Crème had not set the dining table but the coffee table. He had lit several pillar candles, as well as several candles on the mantel-piece, and turned off the lights. The coffee table was set for one and he had tossed the dressing on the salad. Moving closer, Candy wrapped her arms around Caramel and went up on tiptoe to kiss his neck in a thank you.

"Wow, you truly are a wonderful Crème, and Colossal deserves all his special treatment," she seduced.

"Yeah, baby you were acting so ugly when I got here. I'm glad you are excited about dinner. Now, come sit on this pillow until I come back. I want to serve you tonight."

Crème seated Candy on a fluffy pillow from the sofa at the coffee table. He removed the ginger mango tea from the refrigerator and filled two wine glasses. Next, he filled a square plate with veggies and tofu and sat it on the table while simultaneously dropping himself down onto the pillow, spreading his legs around Candy. Pulling her closer to him Crème started feeding them both din-ner. Candlelight and the aroma of dinner pleasantly assaulted Candy and Caramel Crème. Each was deep in thought about their relationship and everything to come in the future.

Candy swallowed a piece of tofu and turned to face Caramel Crème.

"Have you thought about doing this everyday with me?" she asked.

Caramel Crème shook his head in response to Candy.

"Well, I think you make the perfect friend for a sexy lady like myself."

"A friend Candy?" said Shane, asking an unimagina-tive tone.

"Yes a friend, sweetie. We are too old for you to be anything else, cause you are nobody's boy," Candy assured.

"You right about that baby. Now close your eyes, let me feed you, and take care of you for the rest of the evening."

Imani

"**H**ey girlies. Just left Weight Watchers for my weekly come to Jesus with food and points," Imani said. "I don't know about this suicide walk you all take every Sunday.

"Imani, if you want to have a man you need to shut up and get in gear," Shannon replied. "You need to get a trainer and start jogging. You can diet or eat for life all you want. But to get sexy and get a man you need to train. And by training, I mean run for life and a man. When you are tired and can't imagine taking another step, go running, and run like your life depends on it. You want a new friend right?"

"Yes, Shannon I want a new friend, but must you be so damn drastic," said an unconvinced Imani.

"Yes, landing the perfect specimen is a skill. I keep telling you, you need to follow the rules and get on board," said Shannon.

Imani brushed off Shannon's man catching theories. "Whatever, Shannon. What do you have to add, Candy?" said Imani.

"Nothing. I think the rules and my constant dates speak for themselves."

"How are you doing? You haven't mentioned that cutie pie doctor at the hospital lately," Imani said.

"No, I haven't mentioned any men lately," Candy said. "Right now I am focused on my career and dropping a few pounds."

"Candy, you have a cute little size ... you can't be over a size eight. What you trying to be? A minus zero? No man wants a stick," said Imani.

Candy admitted, "Well, for your information I have a few pieces of clothing I'm a little too big for and I want to wear them to Lillian's birthday party."

"Oh," replied a puzzled and unmoved Imani.

"Have you started working on your outfit?" said Candy.

"No, just living in the moment. I go to work, gym, wacky ass dates, yoga and Pilates, more wacky ass dates, hula hoop extension class and wackier ass dates," Imani smirked.

"Well Lillian's party is that perfect opportunity for you to meet a new friend. Now you need to start going walking with us every weekend. After a while you can jog with us. That way you will start dropping weight and all that stomach," said Candy.

Imani was still very unmotivated. Their exercise regimen was a bit extreme. "Whatever. I'm not about to do the suicide stroll at the lake. This twice a week jog from the Seabrook Bridge to Westend is too damn much," said Imani.

"That's too much? Girlie you need to work that body," said Shannon.

"Whatever, my body and I have an agreement. We work out for nice periods of time … an hour, maybe slightly more, but we don't do suicide strolls. Anyway let's walk because I need to go home and cook for the week and pull out two outfits," said Imani.

As the ladies continued on their mission, gradually increasing from a plateau to what felt to Imani like a sprint, they reached a feverish pace. Sweat poured off Imani's body. "Look I can't make it. We are only by UNO and I feel like my heart is going to pop out of my chest. Damn, must we keep this pace?" said Imani.

"Yes, we are on a mission and no pain no gain. Move it, Imani," said Shannon.

"Look, my legs are burning and I have sweat rolling down my back and between my breasts. Ladies, I have sweat rolling where sweat should never be," said Imani.

Stopping and bending over, Imani slowly pulled hot air in her lungs while reaching for the ground to sit down. "You two heifers must be crazy."

"Don't stop now …you need to slow down your heart and stretch. Do you want to hurt all over?" said Shannon.

"No," said Imani.

"Next time you need to finish. Anyway, are you going to wait for us to jog to the end or are you going to take a slow stroll back to the car by yourself?" said Shannon. Though Shannon asked, she knew the answer: each time they would all go out, Imani would give up at the same spot.

"Look I'm going to crawl back to my car and go home to prepare for the new week. Later ladies."

Thursday

T he entrance to Snug's was like going through a maze. People were everywhere. It was unusually crowded for so early on a Thursday. With any hope, one of the girlies was already holding a table for the friends. Snug's had a restaurant, bar, dance floor, and stage area for live music with seating.

Imani turned into the hallway and snaked through the people posted on either side talking shit and looking for the next empty seat. Curving through the hallway, she found an empty chair facing the window and looking onto Frenchmen Street. A window table was the perfect space to watch the street and the people moving around the city. There she sat awaiting her girlfriends' arrival, contemplating events leading up to this evening. Slowly her girls all arrived, breaking the monotony of her thoughts.

"Well ladies everyone is here. What's new?" asked Imani.

"Girl nothing is new. What's new with you? What time did you get here, to be posted in the window? The perfect spot to check all the action," said Candy.

"Just long enough to sip a Naughty Shirley Temple," said Imani.

"Anyway, did you pass Private Joy's coffee shop and read the word of the week?" said Candy.

"Yes, I did and I'm looking forward to many big experiences."

"You are too nasty," said Lillian.

Alexis jumped at the opportunity to correct Lillian.

"Who said anything about nasty, big is a wonderful word," replied Alexis. "The word of the day is big, of considerable size, number, quantity, extent or large; to be filled up, brimming over, of bountiful generous proportions or colossal size."

Candy choked on her drink, Colossal.

"Candy, are you okay?" said Imani.

An embarrassed Candy replied, "I just missed swallowing. I don't know how that could have happened."

"Um hum, big must be a mighty big word for you," said Alexis.

"Whatever, girl. I just missed sipped. Nothing big is going on in my life, just work and dating. Justin has been playing around at the hospital and avoiding my charms. But, it's just a matter of time before he is singing the Candy song too."

"Oh my God, bitch, every week you and Shannon are going save the world with your love life and couchie," said Lillian. This type of conversation didn't really bore Lillian, just reminded her of the lack of big things in her own life.

"Whatever, Lillian …why you hating on your girls? You need to hate on that husband of yours," said Shannon.

"Leave my husband out of this. He is a wonderful man and provider. If it wasn't for him, I couldn't be out discussing the word of the week… Big," said Lillian. She said this and believed it yet she couldn't help but succumb to feelings of truth.

"Yeah, yeah," Alexis said. "Does anybody have something positive to say about another man or big?"

"What?" Lillian stopped sipping her Remy and scanned the girlies saying, "What is that shit supposed to mean? My husband is positive and big." She was now defending the honor of her husband, his manhood.

"Okay, Lillian whatever you say," said Candy.

In an attempt to get the girls back to that happy place, Imani chimed in with a colossal story of her own. "Hey girlies, my last date was big and of considerable size. The let down was of gigantic … wait a minute … it was of colossal proportions," said Imani. "I met him at Wave for some drinks and appetizers," said Imani. "He was gorgeous with broad shoulders, pretty white teeth, Hershey kiss eyes, tight ass body, and ass. I just wanted to run my hands all over his body and nip and squeeze. She grabbed the air, making pinching motions."

The girlies all laughed at Imani.

"What happened? Why are you disappointed? Sounds good," expressed Shannon.

"Unfortunately the Negro was doing what you normally do and just served to piss me off about the state of men and women in America. Well at least in my America," said Imani looking from left to right at the friends.

Inquisitively Shannon chimed in with caution. "What the hell?" said Shannon.

"You know whoring, looking for a female to take care of his ass."

"Okay, Imani slow down and go back what happened," said Alexis.

"What's his fatal flaw?" asked Candy.

"We went to Wave bistro. I started sipping a glass of Monchoff Riesling and he started with a Crown and seven. Next, he asked about my job and I asked about his. He said he works as a customer service rep at an AT& T store at the mall while attending school for radiology tech. Anyway, we kept chatting and eventually he asked me how much money did I gross per year at Counseling Connections. Now that shit was a complete shock to me, since I never mentioned working there at all. Just said I was a counselor for Child Protection. Any w-h-o, he told me I was an all right looking female that he would have no problems escorting me to events and spending time with … if I could support his educational studies. He continued with, and I quote, "You can take care of me and I can make you look good. Girlies, I swear the more I date the more I feel like there ain't a normal Negro left in NOLA or America. Damn, must they all be so fucked up?" said Imani.

The story was met with gasps, murmurs, and disbelief by all women privy to the monologue.

"See? You messed up by not using the patented Shannon system," expressed Candy. "What in the world were you doing out with a mall jockey student in the first place?" said Candy.

"Well, ladies I was walking at the park and he struck up a conversation and asked me to meet him for drinks at Wave. Wave is nice restaurant and bar. I mean who can go wrong with drinks," said Imani. She thought this statement would convince the ladies that she was making herself available or approachable. She believed it would display her positive attitude.

"Your ass needs to slow down and focus on going for walks. I swear you make drinks seem like a marathon date," said Candy.

"Damn, what would dinner be like?" said Shannon.

The girls honed in like bees to pollen. Quickly, Alexis arrived to remove their stingers. "Y'all are going to leave my friend alone; we all struggle meeting people from time to time. Shannon, Lillian, and Candy stop it," said Alexis.

"Anyway what's up with you, Alexis? You never say anything about dating anymore," said Candy finding a new target.

"I'm good focusing on work and living. No man news. Candy what about you?" said Alexis.

Now, it was Candy's turn for the hot seat. It was her turn to discuss her dating regimen. "I already said Justin hasn't been acting right, he told me he had to work but that's not true," said Candy.

"How do you know he doesn't work at the hospital?" said Lillian.

No matter the man, Lillian always seemed to have their back. "What! What! Pussy will save the day is having problems," said Lillian.

"Look you need to stop with the crawfish up your ass and leave me alone.

After all, I don't have a husband trying to run on me," said Candy.

Once more, Lillian delivered a speech her heart could not cash. "Bitch, for your information my husband loves me and only me," said Lillian.

"Whatever, chick," said Candy.

"Anyway, as you know I'm planning a birthday party for myself and I need each of you to help me make it a success," said Lillian. Somehow, Lillian's fabulous planned event seemed to beg a question regarding this professed love her husband actually had for her.

"Have you decided when and where?" asked Imani. "Hopefully I will have time to drop a few pounds," Imani added as she drained the last of her Naughty Shirley Temple and popped another popcorn shrimp in her mouth.

"I was thinking on the way here, it could be a maroon and gold party," said Lillian.

"Bitch, have you gone mad?" said Shannon.

"No it's our school colors and perfect for my age thirty-five," said Lillian. An eager and snide remark awaited Lillian's comment.

"Well, Imani never has plans or dates so I'm sure she can help you make it happen," said Shannon.

Silence covered the table and four sets of eyes focused in on Shannon.

"You must be tripping today," said Alexis. "What is it ... pick on our friend day?"

Shannon continued her attack.

"No I'm just saying if, she focuses in on exercising and not eating she will definitely get a wonderful man," replied Shannon.

"Has something happened we should know about?" said Alexis.

"No I'm just saying," said Shannon.

An aggravated and disgusted, "No I am just saying sip your drink and shut up," came from Alexis.

Shannon

S hannon sat twirling the food on her plate while starring at the man seated across from her. The last few weeks had been filled with shopping, day trips, and all sorts of dining adventures.

"What's wrong Shannon? You are not eating?" asked Derrick.

"Nothing is wrong ... just thinking about those beautiful shoes you purchased and that awesome maxi dress. I am going to look super hot the next time me and the friends go out for drinks at Snug's," said Shannon.

"Speaking of Snug's, why do you go there to meet those non man-having whores every damn week? You have me so you do not need to go every week and get drunk," said Derrick. It wasn't that Derrick disliked the girls; he just wanted to be the only important thing in her life. In his mind, any woman with stable friends and support was uncontrollable.

"Look, whatever, I do not get drunk nor have friends with man problems. My friends handle their own business with men; anyway, we don't go there to meet men. We go to reconnect with each other after spending a week slaving at our jobs. Are you jealous? I think you have the sexiest green eyes on a chocolate man I ever have seen."

"Whatever, Shannon. You do not need to wear that dress or shoes while out with them women you hang out with every Thursday night," said Derrick. Although his comments were based in jealously, Derrick was correct. It was Shannon who proudly spoke of her gifts, not the man who purchased them.

"Fine. I won't wear the dress with my friends. For your information some Thursday nights I have to work, therefore I don't get to hang with my girlfriends every Thursday," she professed.

Derrick waited for a moment before asking, "Shannon, are you happy with us and our relationship?" Derrick slowly sipped his Abita beer and finished his oyster poboy. With each bite, oysters flowed from the bread to the plate. He took another sip of beer and waited for a response.

"Yes Derrick, I am very happy with us. What more could a woman want?" said Shannon.

"Shannon do you like living in New Orleans east?" said Derrick.

"Why Derrick? You don't like my living environment?" said Shannon.

"No, it's just… if you lived downtown we could stroll the Quarters, Magazine, and Canal Street while quickly returning to your home." replied Derrick.

"Well, I'm a customer service representative for a grocery store, therefore living in downtown is beyond my means," said Shannon.

"But not mine. I hate riding out there to visit your home. Will you come with me to look at a little something on Julia Street? Think about moving. That way you will be in the heart of downtown," said Derrick.

Derrick had peaked her interest. "Off Julia where?" said Shannon.

"A couple of blocks from Carondelet Street," said Derrick.

Shannon's eyes began to glisten and her mouth salivated with amusement. Was he really suggesting she move at his expense, into the heart of the posh arts district of New Orleans? That area was always vibrant, and if you were really someone, you had to make at least three trips a week on Magazine for shopping and stunting?

"Yum, Yum Derrick that is a nice area. I just love riding the streetcar through the city," said Shannon.

"See, my baby will be able to walk to the streetcar, among many other things," said Derrick.

"Enough said. Dee let's go!" said Shannon. She could not wait to tell the girls of her latest adventure in Pussy Power.

Candy

M irror, mirror on the wall who is the sexiest Candy of all?

Of course, it's me, Candy thought. One more quick check and it's time to hit the streets. Chanel eyeliner and mascara, pink and gray smoky eye shadow, Mac powder, and nude lip-gloss. Check. Mist of FCUK perfume. Check. Fitted theory jeans, Brooks Brothers dress shirt with French cuffs, multicolor Michael Kors belt, and Prada red sole shoes. Check. Mirror, mirror this girlie is hot. Candy girl you have struck the perfect balance of sexy and chic. Check. Okay, time to step out and have some fun. Shelby, my car, Momma is on her way.

As Candy entered her high-powered toy, she gave it a friendly salutation, "Hey girl. Time for you and me to go on a magnificent ride. Okay, Shelby, let's go find a new friend and check what your future Dad is doing. Her car purred to life, then she quickly cruised downtown I-10 west. Caramel Crème and his fiancée hung out at the Wine Loft, and Candy knew this. She figured it was time to get some much-needed data. There was nothing like a good ole investigation to discover her opponent's weaknesses and then crush them.

She carefully checked the rearview and side mirrors to be certain her surroundings are safe. Slowly she pulled into the crowded downtown garage. The Wine Loft had a great happy hour featuring two for one martinis and wines, so she was sure most cars in the garage were for its patrons. She spotted a seat at the bar and headed for it. Candy sat at the bar on an angle and scanned the crowd.

"Hi, how can I help you?" said the bartender.

"Sure Sweetie. Can I get a candy apple red martini?" said Candy.

"Sure sexy, on the way. Hey what's your name?" asked the bartender as he scanned her body.

"Candy." She replied with a smile.

"Okay one apple martini is on the way." The bartender left and returned within a few minutes with a blood red elixir.

With a gulp, the burn of perfectly mixed apples and vodka slowly poured down Candy's throat.

"Mr. Bartender, excuse me but this is wonderful. You and I are going to be friends," said Candy.

"Well sexy, that is very good for me and the other bartenders that work this section," replied the bartender.

Taking another sip of martini, Candy asked, "Can I have another martini just like this one? Do you have any Caramel on the bar?" said Candy.

"Caramel?"

"Yep. If you have some, can you dip the candy apple slice for the drink in caramel and send it to the gentlemen sitting at the booth on the last row on the left?" she asked. Candy liked to live dangerously, hence the sports car, two men, one which was spoken for. She was a true adrenaline junkie.

"Sure sexy, whatever you want. Do you want to send a note?" said the bartender.

"Nah no notes," said Candy. "But let me settle up right quick. Never know when a girl has to make a quick getaway."

"A drink for you sir," the waitress said.

"A drink? I didn't order a drink," said Shane.

"Well, sir the bartender told me to bring a martini to you." Leaning forward and whispering in Shane's ear, she said, "The lady at the bar said you looked like you needed a martini."

Shane smiled, took a sip, and started to choke. "What is this? God this is mighty sweet for a martini."

"Oh, sir, slow down. That is a Caramel Candy Apple Martini. Don't you wish you could just bite into a candy apple? I swear every time I have one of those drinks, I can't stop thinking about Candy apples. Happy sipping, sir."

Thanks, he smirked. Shane immediately turned and scanned the room. No Candy anywhere. *Her ass is not funny. How the fuck is she going to send me a drink while I'm out with my lady? Damn Candy! What? You trying to get us busted.* Picking up the phone, he dialed Candy, then texted, *I don't see you, but stop. I am out with Nikki and that's it. Candy, be sweet baby.*

"Hey baby. Who you calling?" asked Nicole.

"Oh babe didn't hear you walk up. Oh nobody," said Shane.

"Nobody huh? Hey when did you order the drink?" said Nicole.

"Oh the waitress passed by while you were in the ladies room. She brought me her favorite drink," said Shane. Nicole looked at it with disgust.

"Well, if she's bringing out favorite drinks where's mine?" said Nicole.

"Um, I don't know but you can have mine?" said Shane.

"I don't want your drink. I want my own," said Nicole.

"Sorry, beautiful. This one is for me, but take a sip," said Shane. He offered her the sweet drink.

"Damn, baby this is some good shit. Who ever thought to mix Caramel, Candy apples, and vodka?" said Nicole. Unbeknownst to her, Shane was in the habit of drinking vodka and mixing in some Candy to create ultimate sensation.

"Beats me Nicole. Happy you like my drink," said Shane.

Sliding into her car with a smile, Candy thought, *Wonder what Caramel Crème thinks of his drink being served at the Wine Loft. I hope he likes his Martini. Now, time to find a new friend, catch a set, and sip slow.* Heading deeper uptown, she drove on Tchoupitoulas Street to Dos Jefes Cigar Bar. Buzz, Buzz, Buzz…Candy reached down to read an incoming text message… "Be sweet baby." After pulling into the lot across the street, she got out of her car and said, "Bye… time for momma to find a new friend. Mirror, mirror in the car who is the sexiest of all? Of course me." Lip gloss and hair neat. Check. Candy entered the bar, glanced left and right to scan the crowd. *Okay nobody I hang with is in this spot tonight.* Stepping up to the bar, she said, "Lemon drop please."

"Sure thing miss." said the bartender.

"Thank you. I want to run a tab. I am going check out back," said Candy.

There has to be a hammock with my name on it, she thought, slowly sitting down. The sounds of smooth jazz did wonders for her mind and mood. As she took a tiny sip, she thought, *U-mmm, this drink is wonderful.* At this point, Candy knew it was well time to find a new friend and flirt. *Okay girl got to turn in the hammock slightly to the right to show off your beautiful backside and sexy shoes. There is nothing like a visual feast to make a man lust and wish. Wish away gentlemen and let your wallet become my new best friend.*

"Nice sandals," said the man.

"Excuse me sir," said Candy.

"I said, Nice sandals." he replied.

"Well thank you." Just as she said, the first man was already trying to get some Candy.

"What's your name?" said the handsome stranger.

"Now do you need my name?" said Candy.

"No. I would like to call you something while we chat."

"Call me Sandals," said Candy. She thought she was crafty with her words.

"Look sandals, it's just you, me, some good jazz and a hammock."

"Speaking of hammocks and jazz who is playing the next set?" said Candy.

"I don't know gorgeous. I only know I want to get to know you."

He sounds a bit cheesy, she thought.

"Um," she murmured, taking a slow sip of Lemon drop. "Is that right sugar?" replied Candy.

"Yep that's right. What you drinking?"

"I'm slow sipping a Lemon drop," said Candy.

"Well, let me order you another Lemon drop and Crown and Seven for myself." He was insistent on spending as much time as he could with her, so what if that meant another $20 to his tab?

"Thanks sweetie for the new Lemon drop to slow slip. What's a beautiful display of Hershey masculinity doing in here all alone?" said Candy.

"Just catching a set with a few friends when I got distracted by a beautiful girl. I must say those shoes and their red bottoms are hot."

"Nah baby, Hot is you. Real cute, but what's your name. Are you strange? Crazy? A stalker?" asked Candy, though he wouldn't admit to either of the charges.

"No. No. And No. Look. I just asked you your name twice with no response." He laughed.

"I told you my name is Sandals," said Candy.

Candy looked over her drinking partner and estimated him to be 6'3" with 215 pounds of solid muscle. His hair was faded and neat to his scalp. His eyes were chocolate almonds above the juiciest mouth she had ever seen. *Lawd this man is fine.* Her gaze continued to scan over a beautiful Hershey treat. She took another sip of her drink while making eye contact with the handsome man, who sat across from her.

"What's your name?" said Candy.

"Now you won't tell me your name so, I guess we are going have an interesting time with no names."

"Anyway sweetie, I will just call you King. After all, you just ordered a Crown and Seven," said Candy.

"Well Sandals, I am cool with King." King extended his hand and smiled at Sandals.

"Sandals, is there room in that hammock for one more?" said King.

"Now King, what kind of girlie invites a man to her hammock without even knowing him?" said Candy.

Candy continued to sway and bob her head to the beat as smooth jazz wafted through the air. King slowly smiled at Sandals while tossing back the rest of his Crown and Seven. Candy covered her drink, closed her eyes and let the music wash over her body. The sounds and the alcohol relaxed her body, creating a little buzz. Candy uncovered her drink, took another sip, allowing a soft moan to escape her lips.

"Damn this is good, my King."

"Damn, I shoulda had what you're drinking."

Candy just giggled at King's response. "So what do you do King?

"I go to work." He stared at her, knowing her next question.

"Where's work?"

"I'm a jock for one of the local radio stations. What do you do, Sandals?"

"I'm a nurse."

The stranger thought Candy might be the night nurse of his dreams. "Do you like taking care of sick people?"

"Love it," replied an unsuspecting Candy.

"Well I'm sick at this time and you won't give me my medicine," he flirted.

Candy continued to giggle at the incredibly handsome man sitting beside her at a table. She turned over more in the hammock, reached out for the King and gently kissed him on the cheek and pulled him in the hammock for the rest of the set. "King did you like your medicine?" said Candy.

"Imani I am indoors, and it's been a long week and I am ready to go dance and have some fun. You know I can't be locked up in here listening to all these damn problems on a wonderful spring day," said Alexis.

"Alexis, I don't think it's spring yet," said Imani.

That didn't bother Alexis. As far as she was concerned, the New Year had passed, she could wear a dress and sandals without breaking a sweat or freezing her tail off. For all intent and purposes, it was spring to her. "Look, the weather feels spring-like so it is spring," answered Alexis.

"Whatever," replied Imani.

"Hey, how are you coming with your training?" said Alexis.

"It's okay. I went walking this morning and Shannon and I are going to walk in the park tomorrow. City Park has a new walking trail. The change of pace should be good motivation. I am trying to lose ten more pounds by the Crescent City Classic. The training guide combined with my weight watchers for life should be a good thing for spring," said Imani.

"Okay, Imani. I swear, do you ever stop and relax? You work all day. If it's not listening to too many problems, it's you stressing over the size of your ass. You need to let somebody hit you in the center of your core with his penis and the weight thing will be all over with," said Alexis.

"Leave me alone, Alexis. I have always been a big girl. I just don't want to look like a beached whale trying to find her way back home. Anyway Weight Watchers and walking work for me," said Imani. Imani loved Alexis' support and knew that she was a true friend, but Imani had her goals.

"Anyway I have two more clients before the day is over. So enjoy your early evening. Maybe you will join us for our Saturday morning walk," said Imani.

"Maybe, Imani. You know I can't take all that crazy shit with Shannon and Candy," said Alexis.

"You need to leave our friends alone. Every girlie has to come into her own," said Imani.

Alexis gathered her purse and work bag to head home. "Bye, counselors and therapist," she said. "Everybody have a good weekend and remember to have some fun."

Alexis smiled and waved bye to her colleagues, taking a slow stroll to the elevator and pushing the Down button. Alexis slowly tapped her butterfly heel sandals and waited for the elevator to come.

Alexis got into her car and thought, *Oh my God it must be a million degrees today. Oh, I got to let the windows down and let some air circulate. It isn't even summer and I'm afraid to sit down in my Honda. Lawd, have mercy it's too damn hot.*

She hopped onto the interstate to get off at Esplanade, to the sound of music. Listening carefully, she thought, *Oh no, it's not a second line but who knows … it's spring and I hear a band. Cool, cool it's just some youngsters practicing.* She rolled down her window to catch some more sound. She yelled out of the window to some cute little people, "Baby y'all gonna be ready in a few more years … sound good. Just keeping doing what you are doing and you be will be moving Trombone Shorty out the way and making way for your own band," said Alexis.

She opened the door to her house and lit a candle. She thanked God for Fridays and thanked Him for her Suga, too. As she picked up and sorted through the mail, she saw, bill, bill, a strange envelope, invitation, bill and what's this. Opening the envelope, Alexis looked down on a message.

Meet me at home at 6:30 sharp. I have a few hints for you waiting on my bed. I look forward to you visiting. Baby, bring a change of clothes. Everything else is on me. See you at 6:30 Michael.

Oh, I just like this brother's moves. Well looks like I can take a bath and get ready to enjoy my hints. My hints better be good. She walked through the house and thought. *Bills you can wait. Girl, get in gear you need to take a bath and find something cute to wear.*

As she turned on the water and plugged the tub, Alexis let warm water mix with some Ann Taylor Sheer Peach Honey Bubble Bath. *Okay he has hints and I will smell so good he won't be able to resist my goodies or me. Now for clothes, I can wear my Two Lips Jeweled Butterfly black metallic tee strap wedge heel sandals. Nothing like being Amazonian, my Seven jeans and cute multicolored crochet halter-top. A little skin always makes a man lose focus. All right girlie. Sexy fit and shoes now let's get this bath and get on the road.*

An hour later and she was back in the Honda. It was a quarter to six and she thought that maybe a ferry ride would do her good. Alexis did not want to fight the Crescent City Connection on a Friday night to go to the Westbank traffic. Since Katrina, it seemed like everybody lived on that side. Since she lived in Treme, the ferry was only minutes away. She pulled the Honda on the ferry with a breeze. It was if everybody forgot you could get to the Westbank on the water too. Oh, well her good fortune.

She leaned on the doorbell and carefully posed to show off her great curves and perfect ass. *Thank you momma for all my curves; I may not have liked my curves as a girl but I love when Michael kisses me from my tailbone to the inside of my knee. Who knew you could have erogenous zones on your back, butt, and knees.*

"Hey baby, come on in," said Michael.

"Hi, Suga, A girl is curious; where are my hints?" said Alexis.

"Just like the note said, lying across my bed," said Michael.

Alexis quickly walked in the house and started for Michael's bedroom.

He pulled her to his chest. "Baby did you forget something? Aren't you going to kiss me hello? What? A brother can't get no love? At least a "Hey Suga" rub on the forehead," said Michael.

"Suga, I'm sorry," said Alexis. Alexis slowly kissed Michael hello, giving him a peck for every letter of the word. H-e-l-l-ooo, and a tongue battle punctuating the O.

"Is that better Suga?" said Alexis.

"Yes, that was much better baby. Are you hungry? I can order in some food. Baby come back here and lift up your foot?" said Michael.

"You like Suga?" said Alexis.

"Baby can you walk in them all night?" said Michael.

"Yep. They are only five inches of cut-out, butterfly-edge heel fun. It's worth it just to see the look on your face. But no, I'm not hungry at all. I am going to check out my hints," said Alexis. Alexis was having too much fun and the anxiety in her was rapidly increasing.

"Baby, put your hints on and come here," said Michael.

"Here?" said Alexis.

"Yes walk into my den and model for me. I want to show you the rest of the hints. Oh and sweetie keep the butterfly shoes on… they fit right on in," said Michael.

"I just love it. My Suga got himself a shoe fetish," said Alexis.

"Nope, baby, I just like pretty toes," said Michael.

Alexis entered Michael's bedroom and ran her fingers over his bed. "Oh my. A lace teddy, a Mardi Gras mask, two strands of pearl beads, and some glitter body oil. Where in the world is he taking me now? All these hints suggest Mardi Gras but it's already passed," said Alexis. She stripped off her crochet shirt and jeans and quickly slid into the teddy. *Well Mr. Michael,* she thought, *this*

thing has a thong back. Now where is he taking me? Anywhere
he is trying to go, I'm game.

Quietly Alexis entered the den with a lace teddy having replaced her clothes, with mask in place, and her hair
flowing. One strand of beads rested on her wrist like a
bracelet and one strand hung long on her neck. Candles
lit the room and Michael was waiting in an oversized
armchair. Alexis sat down next to Michael and he quickly
pulled her legs over his and started to kiss her hands,
neck, and the tops of her breasts that were peeking out
from the teddy.

"I just love this on you," he said.

"Where did you find this? It is wonderful. Being a
curvy woman I've never had a teddy fit me like a glove,"
said Alexis.

"Oh that's my secret baby. Let me borrow one of your
beads? Do you like your hints and have you figured out
where we are going?" asked Michael.

Michael gently dragged the beads down Alexis's
body, exiting at her center. He pulled the beads over her
clit while kissing the perky cleavage created by the teddy.
Slowly, he pulled her down to a blanket he'd spread out
over the wood floors. Michael continued to tease her clit,
nipples, and core to no end, using the white pearl like
beads.

"So where are we going baby?" he asked.

"Oh, Suga that feels good. I don't care where we are
going," said Alexis.

Michael continued to pull the beads over her clit
with one hand, while palming her breast with other, all
while collecting quick kisses.

Thank you, Jesus. Oh, Suga that feels to damn good. "Baby don't stop!" said Alexis.

Rolling onto his back, he pulled Alexis on top. "Baby you know what to do, and leave the heels on," said Michael.

"Yeah baby I do know what to do. Let me borrow these for a moment," said Alexis.

Wrapping the beads around Michael's penis twice, she gently rolled them over his member while kissing his tip. She continued licking and rolling the beads over his penis until he could take no more.

"Baby, Baby, Baby!" he said.

Michael pulled Alexis from his penis and pulled a condom off the table. "Baby I want you to take us home," said Michael.

Alexis slowly moved her body over her most prized treat and gently pushed down, allowing Suga's head to push through her tight wet pussy with a quick swoosh. Opening up more and more for him Michael made up for all the night's there was no Suga in the house. Despite the condom, Alexis could feel every mega inch of Michael's Lysol can thick penis. "Oh Baby I love you and this thick dick," said Alexis.

Michael quietly told Alexis she was beautiful while rubbing her arms and holding her to his chest. "So have you figured out where we are going baby?" he asked.

"No. No, I don't know where we are going. I'm still trying to wrap myself around my teddy, mask, and beads. I would guess we were going to Mardi Gras, but since it has passed, I don't have a clue. Suga why don't you tell me?" said Alexis.

"Nope baby. You need to take everything home and think about it for a few days. You are so smart, baby, and I know you will figure this out. Anyway, let's lie here for a few and enjoy. I really am digging them heels baby. How many inches is that again?" said Michael.

"Boy you need to stop. I told you they are five inches. I wanted to get closer to your height. Besides, I know your ass and your likes. You, my dear, love some high ass heels. I will be wearing these again times three. Cause they made my Suga harder than titanium. Oh, Suga that was better than some sweet strawberry beignets," said Alexis.

Lillian

illian walked through the house, visualizing how it would be set up for her party. She needed food setups, floral arrangements, and a bar setup to maximize the party experience. The furniture from three rooms in her and Jared's uptown home would be moved to a storage truck. Highboy and buffet tables needed to be rented. A deejay and band would be booked to entertain the partygoers. The party would require several servers, an overflowing buffet of tasty treats, and two bars. She wanted a bar setup in the dining room at the front of house and another on the patio leading to the deck and water pond. On the entry table, party favors and gold accent pieces would be displayed. The food had to be bite sized and easy to eat to maximize mingling. The party theme was *Golden Time*. All she needed now was a few maroon and gold accents. There was nothing like gold to make things look rich and elegant.

My party is going to be the shit. Lillian busied herself, walking through her house and pantry, making a list of needed party items and items on hand. She planned to serve a menu filled with fun foods, bruschetta, tossed

salad greens with pecans and apple pieces, shrimp cocktail, crawfish egg rolls, lobster pizza, grilled chicken,
stir-fry veggies, spinach dip, Mardi Gras rice pilaf, and a
birthday cake. Two bar setups with theme drinks.

"Jared, my birthday is coming and I'm looking forward
to us reconnecting in every way. It's a good time for us to
get away and celebrate with the girls. Maybe we can try
to get another baby on board. Do you still want a boy?"
said Lillian.

"What?" Jared replied with a dazed look. "Woman
are you serious?"

Lillian's breath caught in her chest. She held her
breath until it burned, forcing her to release it slowly.
"Jared did you hear me?" she asked softly.

Jared's cell phone rang and he picked it up before
Lillian could tell him not to answer it. Turning away
from Lillian, Jared smiled and quietly answered the caller
on the phone. "Talk with you later, Bye," he said. Jared
smiled and ended the call.

"Did you hear me talking to you? Anyway who was
on the phone?" said Lillian.

"Oh, just one of the guys from work," he replied.

"What? Negro, I'm supposed to believe you smiled
to one of the men from work calling you on the phone?"
said Lillian.

"Yes, woman, isn't that what I said? No I do not want
a son or another child with you," said Jared.

"Well I want to spend some time together and make
love," said Lillian.

"Well some sex is cool but I'm stressed at work now
and don't know. I'll see what I can do, woman," said

Jared. Inwardly Jared frowned at the thought of being with her sexually.

"Jared, are you seriously telling me you are too busy to have sex?" asked Lillian.

"Look I have a lot going on, woman," snapped Jared.

Lillian turned around and fixed Jared with a menacing grimace. "Well Jared I know my golden time birthday bash is coming and I know I will be busy, too. Happy birthday to me and tell that Negro that makes you smile you need some time off to make your wife smile," said Lillian.

Reaching for a wineglass and pouring another glass, Lillian smiled to herself, raised a glass, and toasted to having a beautiful birthday as her husband walked out the door. *Yeah Jared, I know you heard me, and your Negro did too.*

Lillian loved her life and uptown home. She had a wonderful, yet busy life, but an unfaithful husband. Lillian rubbed her eyes and dreamed about her golden party setup. The party plan was completed, food and tables, ordered. All she needed to do now was find a super sexy golden dress to turn heads. *Girl, got to stay focused and wow your husband at this party. Lawd knows you don't want to be a single mother like your mother so, everything must go well. As my friend, Candy would say, "Nothing like eye candy to make a man want to take a bite."*

Candy

"Thank you my Hershey King for the walk to my car. I can't tell you the last time I had a gentleman walk me to my ride," she said. "Well you're welcome Sandals. Sandals can I get your number?" said King.

"King, I thought we agreed to be Sandals and King. If I give you my number you will know my name," said Sandals. Candy was convinced she was controlling the situation, as she was mocking him.

"Will I see you again, Sandals?" he replied.

"Of course, King. I come here all the time to slow sip lemon drops, lie in a hammock, and float with some good jazz," said Sandals.

"Sandals, what night?" said King. Still he attempted to get more intricate details and time with the mysterious woman.

"Well King, I will see you here when our stars connect," said Sandals.

"Sandals, do you have a man or something?" he replied.

"Nope, a girl can't be too careful," she said.

Candy got into her car. Sitting behind the wheel of the driver's seat, she turned the key. "Anyway, King good night and thanks again," said Sandals.

Her Mustang purred back to life. She headed east on Tchoupitoulas, turned left at Race Street and right on Annunciation heading to I-10. Candy checked the rearview mirror to make sure King, nor anyone else, was not following her.

As she drove on I-10 towards the city, exiting at Elysian Fields, she thought, *What is happening with Justin? I have never had a man ignore me. We are going to see what's up with his ass once and for all. Well we have had several fun hours of being a treat and giving treats. Now it is time to find out what our new treat is doing. Candy is sweet and everybody loves a sweet treat.*

Candy parked her ride and popped open the trunk, then replaced her shoes with sneakers. It was time to explore Justin and discover why he was ignoring all her skills. She placed her oversized Michael Kors bag in the trunk, and she slid a car key into the pocket of her fitted Theory jeans. She looked out from under the trunk roof, with car keys in place. It was time to go and explore Justin's house and look around for a second time.

Exactly five hours had passed after leaving home to find a new man for herself. *Girl, it will be good to have someone to wax you on the weekend.* Candy strolled down the street in jeans and Nike tennis shoes. As she walked down the street to Justin's, she passed cars, dogs, and few drunks hanging out in front Mimi's bar. Candy walked past the drunks, and down the street to an alley on the side of Justin's house. Tipping to the back of the house, she went to the area where den was. Candy heard a door close as she stood at the back of the house. Justin was home and entertaining some other woman. *I be dammed!* she thought. *How is he going to play me? Candy? Everybody wants Candy. Damn you Justin! Well if you can play, I can play too. I am the only one in this interaction that can have more than one friend.*

Stepping up on a garbage can, she looked into a window and down into the den. She was amazed to see a candle flickering, and she could hear soft music. Scanning the room, she saw that nobody was seated on the sofa. *Damn, him and some moocow must be getting down in his bedroom*, she thought. *Nobody plays me.* She opened the window. Scooting through the window, Candy fell to the floor with a loud thud.

"Justin, Justin, where you at?" she screamed. "What heifer do you have all up in your house? I thought we were kicking it? I mean I had a nice time on our date. What you trying to do?" said Candy.

Justin ran into the room.

Candy looked up into the beautiful brown eyes of Justin.

"Candy what are you doing?" he asked.

A smile eased onto the lips of Candy as she looked into the furious scrunched face of Justin. He was dressed in shorts and a tee.

"Candy what the hell are you doing?" he asked in a quiet voice.

"Nothing... just came by to see what you are up to," she replied.

"Candy at this time of the night, I mean morning," said Justin.

"Yep, just curious why you hadn't called me back yet," said Candy.

Justin stood in utter disbelief. "Candy, are you for real? You just climbed up into my house through a fucking window and your ass is lying in the middle of my floor asking me questions!" retorted Justin.

Justin stared at Candy, shaking his head in disbelief.

She sat Indian style on a geometric print rug and smiled again at Justin, reaching out for his hand. "Justin, I just don't understand why you haven't called me back?" said Candy.

"Candy one more time… what are you doing in my house?" said Justin.

Candy's face slipped smooth as she was questioned by Justin. She stared back at his furious brow and angry eyes and tried to explain herself. "Well, why aren't you calling me back?"

"Candy I have been busy at work and focusing on my future," said Justin.

"Whatever, I know you have some woman in this house," said Candy. Jumping to her feet and running through his house, she began opening and closing every door.

"Girl, are you satisfied?" said Justin.

"Well, somebody must have been here. You want me to believe you were sitting in the house with music playing and candle light all by yourself," said Candy.

"Candy, get out … and lose my damn number. *You are a simple bitch.* I am counting to ten, and if you are not gone, I will throw you back through thru the window you came in and into the garbage can," said Justin.

"Justin, look, I am so sorry. I thought you had somebody here. Let me make this up to you. Maybe you can come over for dinner?" said Candy.

After a night of treats and ill-fated investigations, Candy returned home to plot her next moves with her favorite candy treat. Candy lay back across an oversize giraffe print chair and threw her sexy, toned legs on an ottoman. She played in her hair and rubbed her hands over three twelve packs of condoms lying on the ottoman. Detaching the condoms one at a time, Candy poked holes in every other condom while tossing them into a decorative hurricane lantern. One poke, two pokes, three pokes. Caramel Crème and I are going to be the parents of a beautiful candy crème package. Candy began to sing and hum while pre-treating condoms for her upcoming rendezvous with Caramel Crème.

Shannon

S hannon's bright New Orleans east apartment was hardly identifiable with all the boxes, clothes, and shoes scattered across the floor. The house looked like Hurricane Betsy had swept through. Shannon reflected on her last conversation with Derrick. Derrick had told Shannon that the condo would be ready to move into on Wednesday and that she needed to be ready to move quickly. Derrick was tired of driving to the east to visit Shannon and sit down in her cluttered little space. She still couldn't believe all his jazzy ass comments.

"I will be so glad when you live somewhere worth me coming to visit," he had said.

She was glad the condo would be ready on Wednesday. She needed to work on a new plan to get all of her dreams and needs met quickly.

Shannon was sitting in the living room, packing, and could barely hear her cell phone vibrating on the sofa under a stack of tee shirts. She picked up the cell phone, and holding it to her ear, said, "Hello."

The authoritative voice on the other end demanded to know about her upcoming move.

"Girl," Shannon's mother said. "What's this business about you moving in with a man? Did I not tell you to never move in without a ring and papers?" said Ms. Levine.

Momma, stop it. It's cool. I did not forget what you said. It's that I need to be practical about working to get everything I want.

"You need to stay at your own place or move in here. You need to create a reason for this man to marry you. I mean, did you forget what I said, about riding dick and sucking in your breath until your pussy is tight like a Navigator trying to fit into a Prius. Have you worked your show? Girl you need to make him go crazy while having sex. Do you understand?" said Ms. Levine.

Giggling at her mom's response, Shannon smiled and said, "Momma, I will call you back. I need to pack a few more boxes before he gets here."

"Girl you need to run some bathwater, give that man a bath, and inhale his penis with some pop rocks in your mouth. Don't forget your lessons. Hey and wear something extra special when he comes over," said Ms. Levine.

"Ah right, ah right, Ma, bye," said Shannon.

Shannon sat on the floor and continued to pack boxes and laugh at her Mom. "I swear that lady is a trip. But, the rules haven't failed me yet."

She entered the bathroom, stopped the tub, and prepared for Derrick's arrival. She poured three scoops of Sunburst Ginger bath beads into the running water, and dreamed about her last encounter before moving. She walked through the apartment while the tub filled; she placed some artwork, pictures, and travel reminders in a box. The movers would move everything but her trophies from men in the past. To Shannon there was nothing like a gift to make her work it a little bit harder to get a better gift.

Shannon's hands danced across the last few boxes. Quickly, she filled the rest of the needed materials. *The rest of this stuff can stay here until Derrick retires me from the store and makes me his wife.*

She returned to the bathroom and stopped the running water, then stepped into the tub and slid deeper into the tub, allowing bubbles and scented water to travel over the peaks of her breasts. Shannon dreamed about living freely with Derrick. Leaving the bathroom door open allowed the ginger scent to color the apartment. *Shannon girl you just must make a few more good moves and Derrick will make you a permanent part of his life.* Shannon took a slow breath while slathering Sunburst Ginger body butter from head to toe. She liked preparing for a night of passion with Derrick, it made her smile and plot.

Derrick knocked on the apartment door.

Shannon pulled open the door and watched Derrick glide over the threshold. He frowned at the number of boxes packed and scattered about.

"I hope this is not the way we'll be living in the condo. Girl do you need all this stuff?" said Derrick.

"Yes, Derrick. Do you like the way I look? If you do, then I need my gear and my supplies. Now every time we walk in a room, all eyes hit me and men wish they were you. Baby, what do you want?" said Shannon.

Derrick shook his head and laughed at Shannon and all her stuff. "Girl, I want you and not all these boxes," said Derrick.

"Derrick, stop fussing. A girl has to be prepared for you and our adventures." She replied softly while staring into his eyes.

He agreed, and rushed her out the door. Shannon was overjoyed with anticipation as they got in the car. As they drove off, she continued contemplating their future.

After a quick commute from the east to downtown New Orleans, Shannon walked around the Warehouse district condo in awe. "Wow this place is fabulous! I could get use to living here." The room was bright with natural light pouring in through an open wall of windows. The room had a red sofa, giraffe print rug, crème colored oversized chairs, and tables. A café style table was in the kitchen. The condo had a chic and funky feel. Everything came together as an eclectic mix of style and function. The look of the condo's exterior façade, and the inside were complete opposites.

Shannon watched Derrick walk through the door and quickly go upstairs. While waiting for Derrick to come back downstairs, she moved to the kitchen to make dirty martinis and petite sandwiches.

Derrick entered to the bathroom and took a shower before changing clothes to return to Shannon downstairs. He dressed in a tee shirt and some cargo shorts. Comfortably, he entered the room with a lazy smile and brought his arms around Shannon's cute frame.

"Hey baby," said Derrick.

"Hey yourself, baby. But I am mad at you," said Shannon.

"Girl, I just walked through the door and got settled from work. How could you be mad?" asked Derrick.

"I'm mad because you didn't greet me or invite me to your shower. What's up with that shit? Since when do we not take showers together?" Shannon asked.

"Girl, a brother was hot. My air went out in my car. Anyway, don't talk to me now. I want to chill for a minute and not hear a damn thing," he replied forcefully.

"Whatever, here's your drink with your bitch ass self," said Shannon. "I know that's the last shower you will take by yourself without asking me."

"Mmm... baby these are great. My mouth and lips thank you. But could you leave a brother alone to chill on the sofa," said Derrick. Turning to face Shannon, "Hey Shannon, I am not going to ever be a bitch ass negro... make it your last time saying that dumb shit or you will be sorry. And I do mean very sorry. 'Cause I'm nobody's bitch."

Caramel Crème

"Good evening, Candy. You are glowing and me thinks you owe Colossal a big thank you," said Shane.

"Um, I think you owe me a wow Candy. But thank you for my glow. Nothing like the afterglow of love to make another brother holla," said Candy.

"Candy, do not lie in my bed in my house and start shit. We just finished handling our business" he replied. Slapping Candy on the butt, he said, "Baby get up I need to pull the sheets."

"Why?" said Candy. Although, she knew the answer, she liked making Shane feel guilty, however, he never did.

"Girl, you know I have a lady. Now would you want to come to my house and smell another woman all over me and on my sheets?" said Caramel Crème.

Candy jumped at the opportunity to reprimand him. "If you were doing the right thing you would not be worried about smelling anything but Candy," she replied. She rolled over to lie across Shane's chest and asked, "Baby when are you going to call off your wedding? What's up with all the text messages?"

"Ssh baby...can we stay positive. The messages are to let you know how I feel."

He persisted to pull the sheets from the bed and throw them in the washer. "Candy, come help me make the bed," said Caramel Crème.

"Umm, I'll help if there is something good in it for me," said Candy.

"Candy you already had supper," he replied. Shane felt she should be full from their meal.

"I don't know. Colossal was just okay today. Something, something was missing today," said Candy.

Pulling Candy by the arm and wrapping his arms around her waist, he said, "What was it Colossal missed this afternoon?"

Pulling from his embrace, she said, "We need to get the clean sheets on your bed. Caramel Crème we really work well together, it's taken us no time to fix your bed. Don't you think we make a good team?" She ignored his question.

"Candy stop it," he said with force. Sitting on the bed and pulling Candy's hands in his, he asked, "Why do you continue to bring up Nicole when we are together?"

"I did not bring up your lady. You said we needed to pull the sheets," said Candy.

"What's going on with you?" said Caramel Crème.

"Nothing," said Candy.

"Okay," said Shane.

"I'm just pointing out all the good things about you, and me, and Colossal," said Candy.

"Shane, Shane, Shane baby where are you?" A voice called out from the front of the house using Caramel Crème's real name.

"What is she doing here? This is our time," Candy snapped.

Whispering into Candy's ear, he said, "I don't know. Baby don't start no shit right now. Baby please, work with a brother right now."

"Work with a brother?" said Candy.

"How the fuck is she here now? I thought she was at work? What are you going to do? Because I'm not finished with Colossal," said Candy. This was the explosion Candy had been awaiting. She was ready to make Shane choose ... not realizing he had already chosen. She liked watching him squirm. The adrenaline rushed through her blood.

"Baby please?" said Carmel Crème.

"Shane where are you?" called Nicole.

Yelling to the front of the house, he said, "Um in the bedroom changing my sheets."

"Just put them in the washer." "Be up front in a moment. Grab me a Heineken out the fridge," said Shane.

"Sure baby, you know I can do that for you. We are about to be married in few weeks. You know I got you boy," said Nicole.

"Candy, girl don't start nothing." Grabbing Candy by the arm, he pulled her to the attic door. "Candy, girl, please go in the attic for a few minutes. I am going to get Nikki out of here as soon as possible. Baby, please do this for me and Colossal. Just this one time. Please baby?" said Caramel Crème.

Candy coughed, clearing her throat. "Boy, are you crazy? It's spring in New Orleans. An attic this time of the year is hotter than panther piss on steroids."

"Baby it's still slightly cool outside. It's not like this is May or June," said Shane.

"I know, cause your ass would be married," said Candy.

"Shane baby, I got your Heineken," said Nicole from the kitchen.

"Come on, Candy hook a brother up," begged Shane.

"All right Caramel Crème but this is the one and only time. I am too fine and sexy to sit in an attic, hiding from this bitch to make a Negro happy," said Candy.

Kissing Candy on the cheek, he said, "Baby thank you." A slow smile covered Candy's face. She jumped as the door closed.

Shane pulled the attic door closed quickly, then reopened it and tossed in Candy's purse and keys. Shane rapidly exited the bedroom to meet Nicole.

"Hi Baby. How is my beautiful fiancé today?" said Shane.

"I'm good." Leaning into Shane, she kissed him on the lips. "You just brushed your teeth? It's the middle of the afternoon," said Nicole.

"Yep, ate some popcorn at work. Got a kernel stuck in my gums," said Shane.

"What's up with that?" she replied.

"Umm, Nikki don't you want to hit the sofa and impress your future husband with your kissing skills?" said Shane.

Sitting in Shane's lap and slowly kissing his jaw from the east to west, she asked, "What's for dinner?"

"Sweetie, what do you want?" he replied.

Pulling his lip into his teeth, he waited for an answer.

"I don't know."

"Well, I was going to go to Schwegmann's to pick up a steak and throw it on the grill," said Shane.

Lifting her shoulders, she said, "That sounds good. If you get the grill started, I'll run to the store and grab the steaks."

"Baby that sounds good. Oh get the stuff for a salad while you're at it," said Shane.

"Cool Shane, be back in a flash" said Nicole.

"Okay," he replied.

Girlie are you crazy? How you going to be sitting in a man's attic while he makes plans with his future wife? Are you sick? How good could Colossal be to make you lose your self- respect? Dry your eyes, hold your head up, and leave this man's house and never look back.

Sweat poured from Candy's forehead, down her neck into her perfectly rounded breasts. Candy was drenched in sweat from the heat in a spring attic. Pulling the attic door open with force, she slammed the door into wall, leaving a slight break in the sheetrock.

"Candy baby come here?" said Shane.

"What? No I'm not going anywhere with you." Trembling as she spoke, she said, "You left me in the damn attic for forty-five minutes while you attended to your fiancé. No... there's no way in hell you are going to touch me, let alone hug or rub on this Candy girl."

"Baby please, I'm so sorry," said Caramel Crème.

Candy leaned forward and placed her finger in the center of Caramel Crème's head. "Sorry! Negro, you are sorry for what? Surely you're not sorry for leaving me in the damn attic for almost an hour," said Candy.

"Don't do that!" said Shane. "Candy," he yelled. "Have you forgotten the rules? Baby hold up ... let me make this up to you," said Shane.

"Make up what, Caramel Crème? You left me in the attic to listen to you and your fiancé kissing and making plans to grill dinner. What the fuck is this dumb ass shit? You told me today that it was all about me and us? What the hell is going on?" said Candy.

"Candy it is not like you just found out I'm engaged to be married. After all, my wedding is in May. Look Candy, now is not the time. Nikki will be back in a few minutes. She just went to grocery store," said Shane.

"Oh, now Nikki's feelings can't get hurt? She can't walk in here on us. But, you can come to my home and hold me up when I'm on the way out with my friends. Umm, your ass is engaged when your fiancé might walk in on us discussing our relationship. When Colossal and you are at my house, do either of you remember you're engaged? Well Mr. Crème is this the best you can do? I'm out of here," said Candy.

Candy pulled a frustrated short breath into her lungs and ran to her car. She slammed the door and turned the engine without looking around. Quickly she turned onto the street and drove away from the subdivision. Nobody hides Candy in the attic in favor of his other woman.

In just one, two, three more lights and she and the car would be home.

"Well, my perfect fiancé has another lady running from his home? Who the hell is he spending time with besides me? Well she will not sink her teeth into my sexy baby," Nikki said, sitting in her car, watching Candy drive away.

Shane leaned across the kitchen counter and stared at Nikki strolling through the kitchen to the refrigerator, retrieving steak marinade and garlic. For the next forty minutes, Shane and Nikki worked together to prepare dinner.

"**G**ood morning, Trenell, is everyone in for today?" said Imani

"Good morning, Imani, everyone is here, including your nine o'clock appointment," replied Trenell. This was amusing and disgusting at the same time to her.

"Umm, they are early. Who's on the schedule today at nine?" Imani asked.

"Girl, little miss tie up the entire phone lines with her controlling self, Shay," replied Trenell.

"Well I'm going to prepare my office for the session," grunted Imani.

After entering her office, Imani immediately gathered her note pad and pen, scanned the message stickies Trenell had left, and locked her briefcase and purse in their respective homes. When she was prepared, she entered the client waiting area.

"Good morning Shay," Imani said to her new client. "Can you follow me to my office so we can begin?"

"Good morning, Imani," Shay said as she sat down in Imani's office. "I'm so happy to be here. It's taken so long to get an appointment I can't wait for you to tell me how to work my man. I need him to behave and be more like how he was pre-marriage. Now all he does is sit in front the DVD, Xbox, Wii, and drink on the back porch. Oh my God! I miss my super marvelous man," said Shay.

"Ok, Shay, I need you to stop talking and listen for a moment," said Imani. "I would like to review a few things before we get started. Counseling sessions are confidential unless there is potential harm to self or others. Also, counseling is a reflective experience where we examine our personal choices and develop ways to help us grow. Our session is a fifty-minute hour. We begin on time and end promptly. Do you understand?" said Imani.

"Yeah, I understand. I just need you to tell me how to make my man be normal," said Shay.

"Shay, can you focus?" Imani took a slow breath in through her nose and said, "Tell me about yourself?"

"I am a regional general manager for a chain of restaurants; I make money, enjoy life, and want only the best. I want two kids, a house on Lake Ponchartrain, and a new convertible. I have a sexy husband that was chased after by many women, but he chose me. I enjoy showing him off when I go out," said Shay.

Leaning forward towards Shay, Imani asked, "Is that all you want me to know about yourself?"

Turning her head to the side to stare at Imani, Shay said, "Well yeah. You need to know I make money and enjoy life."

"Tell me about your relationship with your husband?" said Imani.

"We met two years ago. At the time, he was dating several women. But, I had to have him. He was so sexy, six pack abs, clean cropped hair, thick thighs, button butt, and rich mocha skin," said Shay.

"What do you like about the two of you together?" said Imani.

"That everyone else wanted him and I could control him and his circle of friends. I enjoy being the boss and telling people what to do," said Shay.

Briefly, recording Shay's comments into a notepad, Imani said, "Shay, to this point you have expressed enjoying controlling your employees and your husband. What else do you enjoy?"

"I don't know," said Shay.

"Do you have any other interests?" said Imani.

"Interests like what?" said Shay.

"Things that bring you joy and lift your spirit?" said Imani.

"Well, I enjoy going out and turning heads with my husband," Shay replied.

Imani placed the notepad on the table and expressed, "What brings you to counseling Shay? What do you want for yourself?" At that point, Imani had already begun to analyze Shay while attempting to keep an open mind and remain unbiased.

Shay was, however, sounding a bit single focused.

"I want my husband to be the envy of everyone. I want to go out turn heads, hang out with people who like us, and start a family," said Shay.

"Okay, Shay you have no goals for yourself," said Imani.

Shay began to scream at Imani, "Are you listening to me? Down at Chocolates they talk about you like you are a genius. But you have not helped me at all with my husband. Why am I here if you won't tell me what to do?"

Gathering her purse and placing it on her shoulder, Shay said, "I'm out of here. Reaching for the door, she slammed it into the wall, and said, "Bye."

Trenell rushed in to see what was going on.

Imani raised both hands to Trenell in a calming manner. "All is well Trenell," said Imani. "Just going to make a few notes before my next session. Is Alexis here for the day?" asked Imani

"No, she called to say she would be late," said Trenell.

"Thanks, now can we get back to work," said Imani. Imani was bit surprised by her first session, but it was an uplifting surprise. Shay's energy awakened everyone and was perhaps, just what the office needed for an energizing start.

After work, Imani decided to go for a walk to relax. She pulled her hair into a quirky ponytail, placed her bag in the trunk, and started out to tackle Big Lake in City Park. Stride for stride through the park, walking at top speed, Imani focused on preparing for her blind date. She thought perhaps she could lose three pounds by Friday. She thought maybe she could have one drink on Thursday and then walk before and after work with her classes to help shed a few pounds. Now she just needed to find a cute outfit that didn't look like she worked too hard to look good. She thought, *Who knew Anthony could come through on finding a brother for me? Maybe this brother won't have a mommy- manager making his decisions.*

Imani's Danskin gray and yellow Bermuda shorts, yellow tee, sports bra, and tennis all hit the floor with the closing of the front door. It had been a good walk, but now it was time for a shower and preparation for her meet and greet. She wondered if their representatives would hit it off. Imani started her after-walk shower. Tepid water filled the shower along with Tahitian vanilla shower gel. She stepped from under the water spray, onto the lavender bath rug, and slid into a purple robe. She plopped onto the bed, and day dreamed about her drinks with a mystery man.

Girl what are you going to wear? All right, girlie maybe you will enjoy these drinks. Maybe, you will have a friend to brag about by the next Thursday at Snug's. What would Alexis tell me to put on? Hmm let's call her. Imani dialed Alexis, while simultaneously sliding clothes from left to right in the closet. She thought, *Umm, girlie's not answering.* "Hey friend, give me a call back when you get a moment. I'm trying to figure out an outfit. Friend, I'm feeling a little down and I want to feel extra cute. You always know what to put together. Later," said Imani.

Shannon

S hannon slipped her tan fabric Coach bag over her
shoulder and gathered her personal effects from
the Customer Service Desk. Blowing out a shaky
breath, she left the grocery store and headed to her new
warehouse district condo. Having dropped the groceries
for Derrick's dinner in the front seat, she said, "Ohh I'm
too tired and ready for a refreshing shower. Jesus please,
don't let the traffic be too much."

The ride from New Orleans east to downtown was
uneventful. *I miss my apartment. I hate having to drive across
town after working at the store. Girl, you got to start working your show. This Negro needs to step up his benefits package
ASAP. I'm too tired for this shit after work.*

Shannon stepped through the door throwing groceries on
the counter. It was time to get dinner started and she
needed to jump in the tub before Dee got in. Fresh and
free of makeup, and day of work filth, Shannon entered
the kitchen to prepare dinner.

Shannon moved through the kitchen, preparing a
dinner of baked chicken, rice pilaf, and steamed veggie

medley. She made a blueberry, strawberry, and blackberry layered cake with pudding parfait for dessert. She placed the seasoned chicken in the oven. It was time to create the perfect tablescape, using oversized square chargers in red to offset the round cream plates in the center. Square and round candles filled the center of the café table with a soft glow. The napkins were fanned out on the right side of the chargers with utensils inside held by zebra print ribbon. Ding, alarmed the oven timer. She turned the oven off, and left the chicken to warm in the stove. Shannon placed rice and veggies in ceramic pots to keep warm.

"Umm, it's seven-thirty and Derrick is not here from work." She picked up a cell phone and pressed 223-5467. Leaving a voicemail on Derrick's phone, she said, "Baby where are you? I'm at the condo waiting on you." She thought he should be there in a minute.

Shannon entered the bathroom to prepare for an evening of fun with Derrick. She washed her face and arms for the second time that evening, Shannon slathered scented bath oil all over her body and wiped the excess off with a fluffy crème colored bath sheet. She thought, *Manipulation is the name of the game, fantasy is a wonderful thing. I need to be free of work and land Mr. Paycheck.* She changed into an ultra low cut halter dress with no back and only two strings securing its coverage. Lightly she dusted Mac pressed powder over her face, and painted electric green and midnight blue shadow above her almond shaped eyes. Nude lip-gloss added sparkle to her perfect lips. Shannon dusted bronzer on her legs and shoulders to add more sparkle before leisurely lying across a blanket on the red sofa.

Picking up the phone, she dialed Candy to pass time. "Hey girlie. What's up?"

"Nothing just finished masturbating with my favorite toy, Colossal," said Candy.

"Your ass needs to stop before you fall in love," said Shannon.

"Girl, Colossal is great but not exceptional. Anyway, what you up to?" said Candy.

"Just waiting for Derrick to get in to enjoy dinner," she replied.

"Umm, what you wearing friend?" said Candy.

"My patented get everybody a drink royal blue halter dress," she replied.

"The one you wore to the Panther Palace for Alexis' Birthday?" said Candy.

"Yep one in the same," said Shannon.

"Girl, it must be some serious over there. You ass cooking and dressing up for dinner? What ...you ass trying to be like Lillian ... talking about you husband on Thursday nights," said Candy.

Shannon sank into a world of blissful thoughts.

"I don't know, Candy. He is different; I enjoy all our dates, runs, and spending time with him," said Shannon.

"Umm ... your ass needs to get real and admit you like his pockets," said Candy.

"Well they are good too," she replied in a hell yeah fashion.

"Where is Mr. Wonderful?" said Candy.

"Girl I been lying across this sofa channel surfing and talking to you and lost track of time. Girlie, I'm going to say good night," said Shannon.

"Bye and have fun working them rules. You know we enjoy the glamorous life," said Candy.

Laughing at her friend's silliness, she said, "Bye girlie." Shannon wondered where Derrick was. She had prepared dinner, and looked and smelled great while awaiting his return.

Pressing Derrick's name on her cell phone, she said, "Hey what's up?"

"Girl, I got your earlier message. You need to slow up all those phone calls," said Derrick.

"Hey, I only called once," she replied.

"Well that was once too much? Are you at the condo?" said Derrick.

"Yeah." she replied.

"Is my dinner ready? Is the pussy ready?" demanded Derrick.

"Derrick what the fuck is wrong with you?" said Shannon.

"Nothing is wrong … just asking a few questions," said Derrick.

"Can you ask that shit any better than that?" she replied. Shannon was already frustrated from waiting for so long and hearing nothing. Now here Derrick was acting like a pure Derrick minus the 'e' and the two 'r'(s)'.

"I ask the way I feel like it. Do you ask me how to spend my money?" said Derrick.

"Look Bye." Click. Shannon slammed the phone down. Now she was steaming. She couldn't believe that because he paid bills and bought her gifts he thought he could treat her that way.

Derrick entered the condo and threw his keys on the entrance table. Scanning the room, he took in the café table set for two and Shannon sleeping on the sofa. Looking at her pretty dress, flowing hair, and overall glow, he got suspicious. "Shannon, who did you have in our house?"

"Boy, why are you tripping?" said Shannon.

"I'm not tripping ... you have candles burning and the table set."

"Baby, are you okay?" said Shannon. She kissed Derrick on the lips while pulling his jacket off. She beckoned him to come in and relax. "This dress and the candles, it's nothing...I wanted to do something special for my man."

Grabbing Shannon by the hair with a forceful grip, he pulled her body forward to where her eyes were flush with his mouth. "Shannon, who the fuck was in this condo eating dinner at that table? I'm not playing with you?"

Reaching and pushing her head back into the hold of his fist, Derrick slammed Shannon into a wall.

"Baby, stop it!" said Shannon. She wasn't sure whether to become afraid or to return his abuse with her own.

"Stop what?" said Derrick.

"Stop pulling my hair and pushing me, Derrick you're hurting me," said Shannon.

"And you are hurting me." Dropping the grip on Shannon's hair, Derrick turned and sat at the table.

Shannon entered the kitchen and quickly wiped the tears from her eyes. She swallowed down the acid from her stomach with a swig of whiskey. Exiting the kitchen, she placed two platters of food to Derrick's left, along with a bottle of wine. Shannon sat in the chair with her legs tucked under her body.

"Would you like me to open the wine?" Shannon asked.

"Nope, I want you to sit there, eat, and stop asking questions," he replied.

"Okay, Derrick. I can tell you are having another one of your bad days," Shannon said.

"No, I'm not having a bad day. Your ass is asking too many questions. After all, you live in luxury downtown. What possible questions could you have?" asked Derrick. She was simply not understanding that to him, nothing was wrong except her mouth.

"For one thing, where the fuck have you been? How you going to grab my hair like that?" Shannon replied.

"Shannon, shut the fuck up and don't say shit else to me except the pussy is ready," Derrick said through clenched teeth.

Candy

C andy capped the tub and allowed chamomile and vanilla bath salts to perfume the water. She leaned deeper in the tub, allowing water to cover the peaks of her breasts. "Mirror, Mirror on the wall, what am I going to do?" Merlot slowly poured down her throat, helping to create a stress-relieving environment. "I got to get something out of my Caramel Crème. Mainly a little crème. The next time we are together, he's going to leave some soldiers behind," she said. She had placed pinholes in twelve condoms and placed the pretreated condoms into the crystal hurricane lantern on the Jacuzzi edge. *Well the next time you bring colossal here, Mr. Crème, you will be leaving behind a beautiful caramel package. I just got to make sure your ass is mad beyond belief.* She believed there was nothing like angry make-up sex to create a new life. Her experience and knowledge revealed, the more they focused on little head the less they noticed other shit. *Well, little Ms. Fiancé hope you ready for another lady to be in your life.*

Two days later Mr. Crème pounded on the door with great force. Knock, Knock, Knock. He was screaming into the door. "Candy, open the damn door? Why aren't you answering my calls? My text messages? Open the door. Candy, when I come here are you ever going to open the door? Candy I've been here three times. Look, I'm tired of this shit. You knew the damn deal. What the fuck is wrong with you?" said Shane.

"Look Crème, I'm tired, and I am not opening the door. You seem too damn mad with me. I didn't do a thing wrong. You have a fiancé. You had somebody drop in and ruin our private time," said Candy.

"Come on Candy open the damn door." He replied. Crème looked down to a note that forcefully flew from beneath the door. "What? Candy, are you serious? How old are you? Did you really just push a freaking note under the door?" said Caramel Crème.

"Yep," said Candy.

Crème bent down and quickly picked up the note. Scanning the note, he read, "Dear Caramel Crème, it's over!"

Kicking the door, he screamed, "What the fuck is this?"

"A Dear John letter. Can you read? I'm tired and looking for a new love," said Candy.

Puffing out short breaths, he said, "Candy baby please?"

Snatching open the door with force, she said, "What is wrong with you? I've not opened this door for five visits. But, your ass keeps coming back. What's up with that?" said Candy.

"Girl, you know Colossal and I are hooked on your love. I miss you," he replied.

"Now, you miss me, but any other time your ass is representing your fiancé to me," said Candy.

"What you need to say is you're hooked on my good ole' pussy. Let's be honest for once," said Candy.

Pulling Candy into a ruff bear hug, he said, "Baby please let me make this up to you."

Pulling away from Caramel's embrace, she said, "Nope, I'm kind of good Mr. Crème. I met a new friend and I'm sure he will offer me a little dick in a moment."

Caramel Crème's hands tightened into fists and his jaw twitched with frustration and jealously. "Candy do you really want to start shit now?"

Picking Candy up and carrying her to bedroom, he threw her body forcefully onto the bed.

"Let me go" she replied. Kicking and whispering into Caramel Crème's ear. "What are you doing?" Slap! Candy's right hand connected with the left side of Caramel Crème's face with force. Slap!

Blocking all of Candy's future hits, Shane said, "I'm not starting a damn thing. Stop it! Baby we do not hit each other.".

Standing on the bed, Candy pushed Caramel Crème back with her index finger to his forehead. "How you come to my house and disrespect me? First, your ass leaves me in the attic while you kiss on your fiancé and plan to barbeque on the patio. Mr. Crème, what the hell is that?" said Candy.

"Candy," he yelled at her through clenched teeth while pushing her back and kissing her with force. "Candy stop it!"

Walking to the bathroom and grabbing the lantern of condoms from the Jacuzzi ledge, Caramel Crème dropped the container on the nightstand. Candy rolled over, putting her back to Mr. Crème. "Look, I'm not feeling you at this moment."

Kneeling in front of the bed, he looked Candy in the face. "Baby I love you! Please don't do this. Will you open your arms to me and invite me to your bed?" said Caramel Crème.

"Are you seriously asking for pussy?" said Candy.

"Baby, I miss you and want to make it up to you. Don't you want to visit with Colossal?" said Caramel Crème.

Candy looked over the beautiful Caramel colored man kneeling before her. *Why couldn't he drop to one knee and give me the ring?* Candy caught a deep breath in her chest and let it slowly roll out her mouth. Caressing Caramel's face, she said, "Baby I love you. But, a girl has to be realistic. Maybe, our time has come to an end."

"Sssh, girl. You know we are good together," said Caramel Crème. Slipping his hands into her hair and releasing a clip, soft curls surrounded Candy's face. "Girl, I love your hair down, framing your pretty face. You have the prettiest eyes." Pulling Candy's head forward, he kissed her until she grabbed him to catch a breath. His strong muscles could be felt through his button-down shirt.

Sliding her hands lower, pulling the shirt from his pants, she murmured, "Umm, Caramel Crème you feel too good."

Pulling Candy closer into his embrace, squeezing her bottom lip between his teeth, Caramel Crème reached up and pulled down the straps of Candy's sundress. Whispering into her ears, he said, "Girl you are so sexy and hot! I can't get enough of you and feeling Colossal push forward into your tight pussy."

Reaching forward, she pulled Caramel Crème into bed with her. She painted his face with tiny kisses while rubbing his arms up and down along his shoulders and strong back.

Lying back in Candy's bed, Caramel Crème pulled her sundress down over hips, along with her thong panties. Caramel Crème returned the kissing action, painted her body with tiny pecks. He reached into the crystal lantern for a condom and causally rolled a condom down over Colossal.

Candy rubbed her fingers over Colossal's sheathed self and visualized a baby crème. Rolling onto her back with Colossal in hand, Candy guided him home. Kissing and simulating their lower action, Candy and Colossal worked together to create a satisfied Caramel Candy treat.

Leisurely, he dropped his speed and continued to kiss Candy all over. "Damn girl that shit is good. I love it when you're mad at me. You try not to let me make you sing, but in the process you hold your body so tight." said Caramel Crème. "The nut is amazing."

"Whatever, get up and get out," said Candy.

"Girl not that again. You just had the best sex of your life with me and now you want to put me out."

"Look, we agreed not to come in my bedroom, she replied.

"Actually, beautiful, you told me I couldn't enter your bedroom. But, I never agreed," said Shane.

"Whatever, I'm still going to meet my King and make sure he knows I will work hard to be his Queen," said Candy.

Slapping Candy on the butt, he said, "Girl you better stop playing. My dick is still in your ass and you talking about giving my goodies to somebody else," replied Caramel Crème.

Kissing Candy on the forehead, he told her, "Good night beautiful."

"Good night?" Candy questioned. "I think not, time for round two," she answered.

"Wait up, Candy, a brother needs a break," he replied.

With her hands wrapped around Colossal, "I think not," said Candy.

"Candy let me get a condom," said Shane.

"What? This condom in your hand?" Candy asked. Throwing the condom to the floor, Candy started to mount Caramel Crème. "Boy please, Colossal and I are going to be one before your ass is married," said Candy. Sliding down onto Colossal's head, she said, "Shut up, get focused, sleep can come later."

"Candy, wait up!" said Caramel Crème.

"Nope doing what, I want to do. We don't need protection," she replied.

Alexis

A lexis slowly began the suicide stroll while waiting for Shannon and Candy to play catch up. She was about four blocks from the Seabrook Bridge when Candy turned the corner on two wheels. Waving over her shoulder to Candy, Alexis said, "Hey Girlie." The motionless lake colored the background. Alexis' clothes started to gather a little moisture.

Candy ran to catch up with Alexis. She felt a slight burn deep in her legs.

"Did you stretch?" said Alexis.

"Nope, just dropped my phone and purse in the trunk and ran to catch you," replied Candy. "You meant you were going to start on time."

"I waited for you guys twenty whole minutes but, it's not Sunday. So, I figured maybe you two were too busy to manage an extra suicide stroll," said Alexis.

"What's up with you wanting to go for an extra walk?" said Candy.

"Nothing is up ...just wanted to ponder life and clear my head," said Alexis.

Candy looked over to her friend and asked, "Umm, well girlie are you ready to start jogging?"

"Nope, I figured we would walk to UNO, that way Shannon won't have to jog that hard to catch us," said Alexis.

"Well, if she comes anyway. Lately, she has been so caught up with her King Orca Derrick. Girlie, last night she called after preparing dinner for her man. Can you imagine running home to cook dinner and get all dressed up to sit at your own table for dinner?" asked Candy.

"Well what's wrong with that?" said Alexis. That seemed perfectly fine to Alexis.

"Umm, do you have a new man?" said Candy.

"No, I'm just saying give her a break. You know her mom's was a trip when we were growing up. Come on … we were nineteen, and her moms had a demonstration session on how to put on a condom without a brother knowing. Now let's be real, whose mother does that?" said Alexis.

"Well, it is now forty- five minutes into our walk, run time. Are you limber?" said Candy.

"I'm good," replied Alexis.

"Come on girlie let's run. Nothing like a little burn to make your stomach tight and legs perfect in heels," said Alexis. Alexis was pumped and ready for the take off.

"You volunteering to pick up the pace, I know your ass got a man now," said Candy.

"Whatever, heifer," said Alexis.

Alexis' legs burned from the charged-up pace. She was used to suicide strolls, but not at Candy's and Shannon's pace. But, thinking about Mike and all the trips made the burn that much better. *Damn, that brother was so nice. Just where are we going next? I like my beads and mask but really, besides Rio where could we be going? I just got to get used to him and his moves and all the constant love. Well an extra run will help me keep it tight for our next adventure.*

Alexis slowed down and stooped over to breathe in. Her legs were burning from the accelerated run.

"Girlie, don't stop running now. You're almost at Shannon's pace and mine. If you keep our pace you can drop down from a size sixteen into maybe a twelve."

"Girl my legs and stomach are burning," said Alexis.

"Come on let's speed walk so you can focus on breathing and getting rejuvenated for a moment. You must have a fine ass man for your butt to be out here running. Next, thing I know you and Imani will be out here out pacing Shannon and me," said Candy.

Alexis finished doing the suicide stroll and started back for the car.

"Girlie tell your new man I look forward to meeting him," Candy teased.

Alexis said, "What?" as a slow smile covered her face.

Candy repeated, "Like I said girlie, Tell your man hi. Oh, by the way don't be trying to out run the professionals. You can run but a good man will follow and flip the script. You know the deal. I just hope Imani finds a new somebody to go running for."

Stopping short at the Honda, Alexis pulled her purse from the trunk, as Candy pulled her phone and purse from the trunk of her car.

Quickly hugging Candy, she said, "Bye. Good night girlie, be safe. If you talk with Shannon, tell her I'm hot on her heels." Both women entered their vehicles and drove off.

Alexis slammed the door closed. She entered her Treme' home and pulled off sweat-soaked workout clothes while moving through her home, and said, "Girl, you got to get moving if you will make it to Clearview mall for the show at seven forty- five." She pulled out a multicolored maxi dress and gladiator sandals to wear. She thought that would have to do. Alexis quickly showered and changed her clothes to go the movies. Once again, she stepped back out the door to head for the car. She pulled the garbage can to the street to block a parking spot for later. *With the extra run, I won't be feeling like walking up the street after parking away.* She entered the car and headed to Clearview Mall. She spotted Imani and continued driving to find a parking spot. As she parked, Imani met her at the car.

"Hey girl. Did you get the tickets?" said Alexis.

"Yep. But what's up with you?" said Imani.

"Nothing ... went for an extra suicide stroll this week," said Alexis.

"Are the other ladies coming to the show?" said Imani.

"Nope. I did the stroll with Candy," said Alexis.

"What happened to Shannon?" asked Imani

"Don't know. But I will ask her on Thursday," replied Alexis.

The ladies entered the movie theater.

"Are you getting anything from concessions?" asked Imani as she approached the concession stand.

"Nope just finished an extra stroll. My stomach and legs are burning too much to consider trying to eat anything," said Alexis.

"Ok, well you know I smuggled in my own popcorn. A girlie can never eat that million-point popcorn at the show," said Imani.

"Girl, I swear your ass is going to get us thrown out with all them illegal diet snacks," said Alexis.

"What? I bought a diet coke," said Imani.

"Just keep that shit up. I'm not going to movie concession jail," said Alexis.

Laughing at Alexis' crazy comment, Alexis and Imani entered the show.

"Girl check your phone," said Imani.

Alexis pulled her phone out and placed it on vibrate. Texting Michael a quick note, *Suga at the movies with Imani.*

"How was the rest of your day?" asked Alexis.

"A complete trip I need to get away. My new client is trying all my nerves and testing my skills as a counselor," replied Imani.

"Well, you need to call her on the bullshit in the office. Trenell told me about her storming out. Are you really that pushed for clients to accept chaotic behavior?" said Alexis.

"Alexis you work in our practice too. So you are well aware of my client roll," replied Imani.

Alexis turned to face her friend. "Exactly friend. You don't need to tolerate bullshit."

"Anyway, I don't think she knows how ugly her behavior is," said Imani.

"I don't know how not," said Alexis. "Girl, Stevie Wonder could see her manipulating passive aggressive ass." The dimming of the lights served to alter spectator's conversations.

"We will talk later … the previews are starting," said Imani.

"Be right back," Alexis said. She exited the theatre to get a bottle of water. She returned to her seat while sipping the water. "Did I miss anything good?"

"Not really," replied Imani.

Alexis quickly read the message on her vibrating phone. "Enjoy your movie. What about some breakfast?" replied Michael. Alexis quickly texted Mike back, "Sure Suga."

Pulling Alexis arm, she pointed to the phone. "What's up?" said Imani.

"What do you mean?" asked Alexis.

"I mean you have been texting somebody all night. All through the movie previews. Girl, if you had somewhere to be I could have come alone," said Imani.

Alexis held back a blush. Keeping Michael a secret and their affair was becoming a problem. "Nothing like that. Just got a text message," said Alexis.

"Well Alexis your phone has been vibrating all evening," said Imani.

"Okay, Okay Imani. I have a new friend," said Alexis.

"A friend or man friend, because we are too old to be making new female friends," asked Imani.

"I have friends but you are never too old to make new friends male or female," replied Alexis with a smile.

"Does this male friend have a name or should I just read your text messages?" said Imani.

Laughing at Imani's smart-ass comment, Alexis shook her head and smiled at her friend. "He is a friend; I just don't know how important he is."

"Okay, girlie. But from the way you guys are texting... he is very important," said Imani.

Alexis finished her texted message to Michael as the movie began. The ladies laughed until tears ran from their eyes. They spoke of her friend and their crazy ass client. They continued to laugh until the lights came on.

After bidding her friend goodnight after a wonderful movie, Alexis returned home to find a man on her doorstep.

"Hey Lady," Michael said to Alexis as she started up the steps to her house.

"Fancy meeting a sexy brother like yourself sitting on my door step?" she told him.

Whispering in Alexis' ear as she started up the steps, he said, "I figured a movie might have created physical and sexual hunger."

"I'm hungry all right. Just can't imagine eating a bite," said Alexis.

"Baby what's wrong?" said Michael.

"Nothing ...just went running with Candy. She has a quicker pace and today, I caught her pace," she replied.

Michael rubbed his hands over Alexis' shoulder. "So your body hurts?"

"That's the polite way of saying my legs, buns, stomach, feet, hair, and breasts are burning," said Alexis.

Mike scooped Alexis in his arms and carried her to his ride. He gingerly placed her in the passenger seat. Quickly, he snapped her seat belt and walked around the car to the driver's seat. Michael drove down Esplanade to

La Peniche Restaurant. "Sweetie you need to eat something and allow your body to recover from your workout," said Michael.

"I thought my body did that at the show," replied Alexis.

"Doubt it, your body cooled down without a proper soak or stretching to keep your muscles from getting stiff" he replied.

Michael parked the car two lengths from the door, exited the car, and opened the door for Alexis. Reaching in the car to help Alexis to her feet, while, kissing Alexis on the lips, he said, "Time to take care of my baby. Come on give me your hand." Michael and Alexis entered the restaurant holding hands and sat at a window table.

Michael ordered pecan pancakes and garden omelet with pepper jack cheese. He told the server, "We would like some hot tea with lemon and honey."

Alexis smiled over at her dining companion. "Good job Suga. You most definitely are paying attention to what I like."

"I try to do my best," said Michael. "Alexis what are you doing Friday night?"

"Nothing to my knowledge. I plan to go out with my friends on Thursday night, and to Lillian's "Golden Time" party on Saturday. What does my Suga have in mind?" said Alexis.

Pushing the condiments from the center of the table and grabbing Alexis' hands, he said, "Can you get dressed up extra sassy for Friday? I would like to take you to the Melange' Lounge at the Ritz. They have a steppers set at nine o'clock."

Staring back at the man holding her hands, she said, "Oh my god!" B*reathe in and out. One, two, three. Girl, answer the man.* "Sure, Suga. I would love to go. I'm more than willing to wear a sassy dress. Boy you giving me a reason to take another suicide stroll tomorrow."

"No more suicide strolls until Sunday. I want you to be able to dance. Besides, I love your curves. All this running will get rid of my favorite hips," said Michael.

Making a gurgling sound deep in her throat, Alexis said," Better be the only hips."

Kissing Alexis to end the conversation, Michael said, "Baby our food is here let's split."

"Sure," said Alexis.

At Alexis' house, Michael parked in a spot behind Alexis's car and then walked around his car and pulled the door open. He lowered his head and gently kissed Alexis. Alexis could not stop the smile that filled her face. "You're getting to be addictive," said Alexis.

Picking Alexis' bag up from the floor, Michael placed it on her arm while taking the keys for the door. He opened the door for his lady, then he allowed Alexis to enter inside and disarm the alarm. "Are you going to set it for stay mode?" said Michael.

"Hadn't planned to, Suga you're here. I am too tired to get up to handle the door in the middle of the night," said Alexis.

"No worries sweetie, I don't plan to leave until the morning light," he replied.

Turning to look at Michael, Alexis replied, "In that case, I most certainly will set the alarm."

With the closing of the alarm panel, Mike pulled Alexis into his arms.

Alexis' mounds of breasts pushed forcefully against Michael's chest.

Michael picked her up and carried her through the house to the bed. He laid Alexis across the bed as he undressed to enter the shower. He threw his clothes across the chair, then started the water to take a quick shower. "Baby, light a candle and I will be back with you in a minute," said Michael.

Alexis pulled back the sheets, closed her eyes, and looked at the ceiling. "Jesus don't be playing with a girl like this, this man is too good to be true. Please don't let him be a buster." Alexis lit the candle on the nightstand and anticipated Suga's return.

When he returned to the bed damp from the shower, Michael slowly kissed Alexis' beautiful face. "Girl you are so sexy and exquisite," said Suga.

"Umm, I love the way you tell me how beautiful I am. I've never had a man so complementary," said Alexis. Pushing forward to deepen the kiss, Alexis could not control her response to Suga. Soft moans filled his ears and forced him to work harder to hit the correct spot. Thick chocolate legs wrapped around his back allowing him to drop lower and lower into the center of his sweet pot. Mike continued to kiss Alexis, letting her know, "It most definitely was going to be an exquisite night.

Thursday

C andy plopped down in the last chair at the table. "Greetings ladies, why aren't we drinking?"

"We are thinking about our choices. Where did you park? Did you read the word of the week in Private Joy's window?" said Lillian. Candy didn't know which question to respond to, so she focused on the later.

"What's the word?" Candy asked.

"The word of the week is sweet," said Imani.

Rubbing her hands on her face, Alexis said, "Pleasing to taste, not sour or stale, delicately pleasing to the tongue, eye, and ear."

"Well, ladies that sounds like an awesome drink, what are we having?" said Candy.

"In honor of sweet taste on our tongues, ladies tonight's first drink should inspire sweetness. Okay, I'm about to walk across the room and greet Joe with our orders. Roll call time, ladies give me your orders. I'm having a Berry medley mojito," said Imani.

"Alexis?"

"A Red Royal," replied Alexis.

"Candy?"

"Caramel candy apple martini," said Candy.

"Lillian?"

Lillian turned to Imani and replied with a smirk, "I don't drink sweet Remy Martin neat." Lillian was always so disciplined.

"Shannon?"

"Girl, are you tripping? She's not here. How you trying to take a drink order for someone who is not in the house?" said Candy.

"Damn, our late crabby friend is here but Shannon isn't. Umm did you call her?" said Imani.

"Nope, she too damn caught up working a man to hang out," replied Candy.

Alexis grabbed Candy's arm, pulling her friend to the left. "Are you all right? You sound like you're hating on a girlie."

"Naw, it's nothing like that. It's just she doesn't kick it or meet up for runs anymore," replied Candy.

"Have you thought maybe, she's in love? Or even that she may have had an accident. Did you call her?" asked Imani.

"Now you're on the call her thing. It's Thursday. Thursdays equal Snug's, drinks, and looking out for outstanding men," said Candy.

"Whatever, loose the crawfish up your ass and call your damn girl," said Alexis. Imani and Alexis were not feeling Thursday night without their complete group. Candy, on the other hand, felt a bit dissed by their girl for a man, that did not sit well. Candy was not going to let that ruin her evening.

"Imani darling what you waiting on, Joe is waiting on our orders," said Candy.

Imani turned to Candy and replied, "I'm waiting on Lillian to pick a sweet drink."

"I did pick a sweet drink. Remy Martin is pleasing to my tongue and palette," said Lillian.

Tapping the glass on its side, Tap, Tap, and Tap. "Ladies I would like to discuss your respective duties for my golden time birthday party," said Lillian.

"Duties?" replied Candy.

"Did you say duties?" said Alexis.

"Yes to ensure the pleasure of my guests and myself, I want each of you to work to make my party a success," said Lillian.

"I swear your ass is a trip. The first time we come here and you don't fuss about our spirit stop. Your ass has job duties," said Alexis.

Imani returned to the table with sweet spirits on a tray. "Okay ladies I have our first round." She slid into her seat and passed Alexis a Red Royal, Candy a Caramel Apple martini, and Lillian a Sugared Ginger Rum Punch.

"I didn't order this, Imani," said Lillian,

"Oh girl, we were ordering sweet and a Remy Martin neat is not sweet. Anyway, take a small slip, Joe recommended that drink. After all, he is a wonderful bartender," said Imani.

"Girl this is delicious." Lillian turned and looked at each of her friends. "Ladies, I need you all to work and support my birthday event. So far, I've planned to rent a U Haul truck to hold my extra furniture from inside the house. I plan to empty the downstairs of furniture, replacing it with café tables in the den and on the deck. In the formal dining room, I plan to setup buffet tables in an "L" shape to place food. Outside on the deck will be a mini clear tent to cover my birthday cake. The menu is crawfish bruschetta, tossed salad greens with pecans and apples, shrimp cocktail, crawfish eggrolls, lobster pizza, grilled chicken, stir fry veggies, spinach dip, and Mardi Gras rice pilaf."

"Whew, that's a lot of food. Who are you feeding? It's your birthday and you're cooking that much food? Girl on your birthday it's about partying and dressing cute," said Candy.

Wrapping her fingers around the glass and raising it to her lips, Alexis took another sip of her Amaretto and Crown Royal. "How many people do you expect?"

Lillian looked around at her friends gathered at the table and replied, "Maybe seventy -five. It's been a minute since we had guests. So I took this opportunity to invite all our family and friends. I sent out one hundred and twenty invites."

Imani angled her head to make direct eye contact with Lillian. "Are you sure you want to keep this party at your house? That seems to be a lot of people to have in your home."

"Well with tables and chairs plus tables in the yard it should be okay. I will be using the living room for a dance area with a deejay set up. I'm only leaving one couch in the living room nook overlooking the water fountain," said Lillian. Candy stressed that she had no intentions on working, but receiving as much attention as possible. She wanted to work the crowd and nothing else.

"What do we have to do because I personally planned to look for a new friend the night of your party? It's perfect time for me to wear this yellow multi colored halter top with some sassy shorts and sexy heels. Having to work for your party can't interfere with my outfit," said Candy.

Her comment was ignored, but not answered.

Lillian gave a small smile to her friends and started the duty assignments. "Alexis I need you to make a vegetarian appetizer. I will be making spinach dip so maybe a bean dip. Candy, I need you to set up the theme drink bar, which will be self -serve. Imani, need you to set up the tent for the birthday cake and the favors at the entrance foyer. Shannon, can help me set up food and decorations. I had the house cleaned earlier this week, so we can touch up any last minute details. I have prepared and frozen all the food that could be prepped."

Shannon took several steps and leaned over the table to give everyone air kisses, then said, "Hey girlies Sorry I'm late ladies. What did I miss?"

"Just our sweet drink of the night and Lillian giving us our duties for the golden time theme party," said Imani.

Candy sniffed in air and pulled a strand of hair behind her ear. Candy asked, "Where have you been?"

"I'm sorry girlie, I know I'm deep down on your shit list. But, keeping up with a house, work, and Derrick is beyond me. If you could have heard him fussing and complaining about me coming here tonight, you would swear he was a madman in open court. He got so angry because I wanted to come to Snug's and hang out with you all," said Shannon.

"What did you expect? You're living with a man that is paying your bills," said Lillian.

"I expected him to trust that we are in a committed relationship; that I keep our condo together. When I met him, we were kicking it every Thursday. So today's events are not new or different. He needs to get his shit together," said Shannon.

"No, you need to get your shit together," said Lillian.

"What do you mean?" said Shannon.

Alexis took a sip of her drink and pursed her lips. "Are you serious Shannon? Come on friend, you know you work at the grocery store and are constantly looking for a man to take care of you."

"What's wrong with that?" replied Shannon.

"Exactly my point, the man is jealous. You need to slow up the "mommy" tool kit," said Candy.

Shannon shook her head and laughed at the girlie's. "You know my mom keeps a man."

Candy stood and took leisurely steps to the bar. "Hi Joe. Can you send the man in the sky blue shirt an apple martini?"

"Sure Candy" said Joe. "Do you want a note with it?"

"Nope," said Candy. "Joe can you send another round to our table?"

"What's happening ladies?" said Corey.

"You're just getting to Snug's for the evening, "said Alexis.

"Yes madam, we were down at Kings and Queens Barbershop."

"You don't look like you got your hair cut," said Lillian.

"Girl, your ass been married too damn long. I got my hair cut. But going in order to laugh at Mr. Edward at the barbershop is perfect entertainment. He is so crazy. Tonight he was in shop talking about when it's time to leave her," said Anthony.

"Well Anthony ... when is it time to leave your woman?" said Imani.

"According to Mr. Edward, when you up cooking at four in the morning outside, when you drink a fifth of liquor daily, and most definitely when you want to eat over fucking."

"He was talking about his young neighbor who sits outside playing the blues on the deck with the grill going at four in the morning," Corey said.

The girls sang, "Damn who's out eating barbeque at four in the morning?"

"Well ladies a very miserable man," answered Anthony.

"See, you need to try a big girl and a little less trophy. That way you won't need to be the butt of barbershop gossip," said Alexis.

"They have more drama in Kings and Queens than in Chocolates with Coco," said Candy.

Although, he thought it sounded cool and honest, Anthony's next comment was very politically incorrect.

"Whatever, it's more fun tossing little girls around. Besides you ladies don't go out of your way to please a man," said Anthony.

"Oh no you didn't go there. Leave the table and join the boys at the bar." Alexis fixed Anthony with twisted lips and pointed towards the bar. "Please go ... while you can leave. Tell them "Bye" ladies," said Alexis.

"Well, ladies in honor of Lillian's thirty-fifth birthday celebration, I pulled a few strings and got us a table at the Panther Place for tonight," said Candy.

"Candy who did you promise a date to get us a table on a second Thursday of the month? Is it still the owner's night to perform?" asked Imani.

"Well no promises were made. I just called and got a table several weeks ago. We have the center stage table in the lion's den. That way we have the perfect spot to view the Jaguar corner, Lion den stage, and Big Cat Sun Perch," said Candy.

"What?" said Shannon.

"Shannon, why are you tripping?" said Candy.

"I'm not tripping. It's just that Derrick didn't want me to come out with a group of man- crazed women. I refused to give in to his demands but, now you girlies all are planning to end our evening in the Panther Palace?" said Shannon.

"Shannon, we have gone to Panther Palace before. Stop acting like a penis is going to hit you in the center of your forehead. After all, it's Lillian's birthday. She enjoys watching the strippers. Is it going to kill you to watch a few old strippers take off their clothes to some music? It's not like somebody going to barbeque his dick on stage at four in the morning," said Alexis.

"Besides I came out with my singles in anticipation of going to the Panther Palace, and I didn't book any early clients in order to get my party on," said Imani.

"Look ladies, I can't go," Shannon said.

"What did you say?" said Candy.

"Look girlies, I like my situation with Derrick. So I can't do anything that will make him trip," said Shannon.

"Okay, Shannon. But, watching a little dick has never hurt anybody," said Imani.

Shannon missed being with the ladies but was not about to find a reason to witness Derrick's temper again. Something about this temper did not sit right in her mind. Besides, who knew what might cut her off from the money and goods. She lived in the Warehouse district; people worked for years and still could not afford that kind of luxury.

"Okay, ladies let's pile up in Lillian's SUV, that way we can catch the last three shows. The added benefit is we won't have to look for parking for everyone's car," said Alexis.

A lexis pulled out a glazed almond, cold shoulder, A-line dress from the closet. She paired it with three-inch, Steven Madden, Orange, multi-colored, embellished satin pumps to complement the orange and red flower imprinted on the snugly fitted dress. For accessories, she wore a multi-colored, raised flower cuff bracelet with diamond stud earrings.

She picked up the phone and dialed Counseling Connections. "Good Morning Trenell" said Alexis.

"Hey," Alexis said to Trenell.

"Tell Imani I will be in later. I have several sessions midday. Also, ask her not to add any extra people to her evening schedule. I made us some appointments to get our eyebrows and nails done. Pass her a note between clients. We see Roxxy at three forty- five. Also we have manicures and pedicures at five o'clock."

"Okay I will let her know about the appointments."

"Thank you, Trenell. We have to get started on preparing for Lillian's birthday party. Lawd knows what we have to do for the 'Golden Time event."

Alexis jumped out of the car and started gathering up her purse and workbag. *It is time to prepare for my evening with Mike. Well, got my eyebrows, nails, and toes done. I'll get my hair done tomorrow before the party, that way whatever fun is had tonight won't matter. I'm getting my hair done for the party anyway.* She filled the tub with Amber bath salts and warm water. Slowly Alexis washed her body, and continued to prepare for a night of fun at the Ritz Carlton. She stepped out of the tub and patted dry with a fluffy towel, then slathered on lotion and gold dust to make her skin sparkle. Finally, she slipped into a robe to put on makeup and comb her hair. Alexis daydreamed about her date.

Alexis danced in her bedroom while sliding into a super sexy dress as requested by Suga. *If all he wants is for me to get dressed to go dancing then, I have no problem meeting his demands.* The ebony dress gave the illusion of having on no clothes at all. The dress was sexy and shy at the same time. One vibrant flower colored the left side of the A-line skirt. The flower contained shades of purple, orange, red, and yellow. The dress skimmed the knee, allowing for movement. The multi-colored shoes complemented the dress and made all the colors more vibrant. Alexis placed her jewelry on and stared at her reflection in the bathroom mirror. *Wow, girlie you look hot and sexy. Shannon and Candy may be on to something. That extra run has allowed me to wear a super sexy dress without rolls or bumps.*

Michael walked up the stairs and stopped cold when he saw Alexis and her outfit. "Girl you look absolutely beautiful." Mike extended his hand and spun Alexis around. "Girl your dress sways in the air as you move." Leaning forward and kissing Alexis on the cheek, he said, "Baby, I like your outfit."

"Thank you Suga. I hoped you would approve. We should be going, Suga."

"We're good sweetie. Our reservations are for nine. The set normally starts about fifteen after.".

Alexis grabbed her gold clutch and passed her keys to Mike to lock up. Mike opened the car door for Alexis, kissing her on the exposed shoulder before walking around to the driver's seat. After snapping his seat belt, he leaned over and kissed her again. "Girl you look simply beautiful. Baby you look so good, I love your dress, and I'm loving your curves in this dress."

She turned to the left and smiled at Mike.

They entered the club and were quickly shown to their table. Mélange lounge had a dance floor in the center with couches and chairs surrounding it. Tables requiring a reservation flanked the back of the dance floor. The lounge was decorated with colors of taupe and grays and soft muted tones. A live band played on the stage; the music could be heard throughout the club. A waitress brought over an artisanal cheese plate and Mike ordered two ginger martinis. The food was delicately placed on a plate and was a delight to the tongue. Mike leaned over and whispered in Alexis' ear, "Having fun yet?"

"Suga you are making a girlie struggle. I've never had a man be so good to me. And yes, I'm most definitely having fun. This spot is so romantic. What made you want to bring me here?"

"Well Alexis, you haven't introduced me to the girlies. To my knowledge, no one knows we are together. I just wanted to go out with my lady, have fun, and act like a unit in our city. Sweetie, we only hang out when we are out of town," Mike said worriedly.

"Suga, can we dance? I want to move with you. Nothing like showing off my dress and man at the same time." Alexis reached over and placed her hand in Mike's larger one.

"Okay gorgeous. We can dance, but we will also talk about us."

Dancing to the beat and showing off intricate footwork with Mike was beyond sexy and cool. Mike was slowly making up for all the brothers that didn't come anywhere near to being romantic. *Girlie it's too nice just having a companion, someone to go out with, make love with, and enjoy life with. Oh shit, girlie this man might be a problem.*

After hours of intimate dancing and romantic conversation, Michael and Alexis returned home to complete their evening. Upon completion, the two drifted off into a catatonic state.

"Good morning gorgeous," said Michael.

"Good afternoon Suga," said Alexis.

"It's after noon, so sweetie I guess you are correct. Leaning over and gently pressing a kiss to Alexis' swollen lips, he said, "I'm corrected sweetie, Good afternoon."

Letting a slow breath cross her lips, Alexis said, "Suga let me get up and brush my teeth. I don't need to have day old breath with my man."

"Girl, I'm not worried about your breath. Last night was awesome. What's up with all the tricks?"

Spitting out excess hot water and gargling with some mouthwash, Alexis stared at Mike. Umm, exhaling a breath, she said, "Suga; yesterday was the most beautiful day of my life with a man. Lately things between us are unbelievably sexy cool. I just don't know what to make of it. Everyday I keep waiting for Mr. Mike Hyde to jump out. I like your representative to this point; I just wonder when I'm going to meet the real Mike."

"Sweetie you need to relax and stop trying to analyze everything. I'm a man. You are my woman. I enjoy us together. Is that enough for you? Because it's enough for me," said Mike. Mike turned to Alexis and asked, "Alexis when are you going to introduce me to the girlies?"

"Suga, I don't know. The man thing isn't always cool in my friend circle."

Alexis slowly walked back to her bed. Sitting on the edge, she said, "Mike are you hungry?"

"Nope, you are not getting away from our discussion. Besides this weekend is not about you working. It's about you enjoying your man and realizing I'm here to stay. Now will you get dressed?" Reaching forward and pulling Alexis down onto his chest, he told her, "I love you Alexis."

Jumping up from the bed and running to the bathroom, she replied, "I love you too Suga."

"Alexis you don't have to say it, I know you love me. Baby get dressed I want to go to a late lunch," said Mike.

Alexis went out of the bedroom and into the shower to scrub her night off. Leaning back onto the shower stall, Alexis lathered her body from head to toe in coconut craze shower gel. Turning the faucet to the left to cool the water, Alexis splashed cool water on her face.

Her bathroom door swung open with force. Mike stood in the door and asked, "Sweetie are you going to hide in here all day?"

"No Suga I'm just about to come out."

"Oh, I thought I would have to join you in order to get a shower."

Alexis walked across the bathroom. As she reached Mike, she quickly stepped up on tiptoe to kiss him on the cheek. "Go take a bath. I'll be dressed when you get out."

Stepping in front of the mirror to fix her face, Alexis considered what to wear. *Where are we going now? We've been everywhere in the last few weeks. I just hope none of my friends walk up on us. I guess I should consider introducing Suga to my friends. Last thing I need is for Shannon or Candy's ass to walk up on Suga and start the Shannon system.*

Grabbing a pink, white, and gold maxi dress from the closet, Alexis slid it over her head. Catching the right side of the dress between her fingers to tie a small knot, Alexis placed a light coat of sheer daiquiri lip-gloss on her lips followed by a mist of coconut craze sheer mist on arms and legs. Then she stepped into and hooked a pink Badgley Mischka ruffle flower sandal in blush with a gold heel. *Well at least dating Mike has allowed me to buy and wear some sexy ass shoes. Who would have ever pictured me in heels every day, especially high heels; then a shoe with a flower covering the whole shoe with only two tiny straps to hold your foot in place?* Exhaling a small breath and blowing a kiss in the mirror, Alexis stared at her soft appearance. *Girlie, you need to get it together. You are starting to act like*

Shannon and Candy. Lawd have mercy, this man is going to break you.

Mike stepped from the bedroom, dressed in some khakis and polo shirt. "Sweetie you look good. I'm two for two. Two days and two beautiful dresses on my beautiful woman. Sweetie how about some seafood at Landry's? Nothing like sitting on the lake watching the sun dance on the water and in your eyes," said Michael.

"Alright, Mike what do you want?" said Alexis.

"Me? Want? Baby girl, I just wanted to enjoy myself with you," said Michael.

"Suga, last night and today have been great but I need to get moving. Tonight is Lillian's birthday party and all the girlies have responsibilities. Besides that, I need to go get my hair done. As it stands, I've lain in bed with you and played until my lips hurt and my legs burn from you and the loving," said Alexis.

"Speaking of the party, is that an invite?" replied Michael.

"Sorry, Suga I can't invite you to someone else's party. But, I will invite you to one of our gatherings," replied Alexis.

"When Alexis?" said Mike.

"I don't know Suga. Right now, we need to eat so I can be a good friend. Later tonight I can be a good woman to my man," said Alexis.

Lillian

illian strolled to the kitchen to start breakfast. "Get up little ladies. Today is mommy's birthday. We need to get moving. Come have a seat at the table and eat." Lillian placed a platter of scrambled eggs, crisp turkey bacon, and grits on the table. "Little miss put your feet on the floor and move it. Young lady you better be to the table by the time my kettle whistles." Turning to fill a pot with water to start tea, she said, "We need to be on schedule ladies. Your clothes for my party are hanging on the closet door. The movers will be here for nine a.m. to move out furniture. I need you ladies to eat and then go get ready. I need to drop you off at Chocolates to get your hair done."

She pulled the car from the gate. "Get in ladies. We need to get our move on so you two will be on time to get your hair done. Little ladies you can have curls or a cute ponytail. After, I talk with the movers and Auntie Imani I'll be there to get my hair done," said Lillian.

Lillian pulled into a parking spot in front of Chocolates. "Hey Coco How you doing this morning?" asked Lillian.

"Happy birthday lady. I would have thought your husband would bring the girls today," said CoCo.

"Nope. He's at home waiting on the movers. Look, I want the girls to have some cute curls or maybe a ponytail. Girl, you know I trust you. I will be here about one to get my hair pin-curled. Anyway, Coco I got to get going to meet the movers and prepare for the party. You are coming tonight?" asked Lillian.

"Oh, yeah," replied Coco as she waved goodbye to Lillian. "I'll be at the gathering tonight."

Lillian laughed at Coco as she dialed Imani. "Hey girl, what are you doing? Imani what time are you coming over today to help set up?" asked Lillian.

Rolling her head to hold the phone on her shoulder, Imani spoke into the phone. "I planned to come over about six-thirty. I am responsible for the entrance foyer and cake tent. Girl, your birthday cake can't go out to early or it will melt. Are you okay? Did you forget we live in New Orleans? Where it is hotter than panther piss on a spring day?" asked Imani.

Laughing at Imani, Lillian said, "No" silly. I did not forget. Just come early if you can. I need help."

"All right, Lillian. I will be there. But, I have to dip out and come back. I plan to wear a cute little outfit to your gathering. Maybe, I will find a potential new friend. Later girlie," said Imani.

"Later," said Lillian.

Lillian pulled up to the gate. "Hi guys. Why are you just sitting outside on the steps? Did you ring the bell?" asked Lillian.

"Oh yeah, Ms. Lillian. But nobody answered," responded the movers with a shoulder nod.

"I'm sorry. My husband must have fallen asleep." Turning to open the gate for the movers, she said, "Sorry again."

Lillian inserted the key and unlocked the door, then called out, "Jared, Jared. Where are you?"

"What?" Jared shouted. "Woman I'm in the bed. Why are you yelling? I'm trying to get some sleep. I'm tired."

"Jared, our families will be here later. The movers were outside waiting to get in. Did you forget the people are bringing the table and chair rentals at ten thirty?" asked Lillian.

"Nope, but this party and all this shit is your idea. Therefore it should be your responsibility," replied Jared.

"Negro you need to get it together and help out. I'm not afraid to cut up and show out. Jared we've been married too long for you to be acting so selfish. If you left all the women in the street alone, you would have energy to help me with the party. Anyway, our parents, our neighbor the senator, Judge Charbonnet, and everyone who is anyone in the city will be here. Jared I like our home, money, and social status. I will not allow you and your tricks to ruin the luxury lifestyle we have," said Lillian.

Shaking his head from left to right, he said, "Lillian can you please stop all the fucking nagging. You make me sick. Woman you keep saying this and that about women and me. Look, I have friends, however, I'm married. Is it you having an affair?"

"Jared you need to get it together, husband. I'm going to start my morning tea and prep the food for tonight."

Lillian entered the kitchen and started a kettle of water to boil. Dropping a bag of Oolong tea into a cup, Lillian slowly released a breath. *I need peace today. It's my birthday. I want to have fun and enjoy my life,* she thought as she added boiling hot water to the cup, followed by honey. *I hope this can settle my nerves.*

Lillian returned to the kitchen after giving the movers the final list of pieces to move. She moved to the refrigerator to pull out supplies to get started cooking. She placed the food deliveries inside to chill. Lillian chopped spinach, onions, and other veggies and added marinade to the chicken. Turning the bubbling rice off and draining excess water off, she slowly added grilled chopped eggplant, squash, and zucchini to cooked rice. The rice mixture filled the circular chafing pan. Then she set up circular chafing dishes on buffet tables.

"Hey ladies! Thank you again for coming early to set up. Has anyone talked to Alexis? She is not here," asked Lillian to the other friends.

"Lillian calm down. I'm here, Candy is here, and Shannon is here. We can set up the food, cake, and favors. Will you shut down all the party planning and go take a bath and get dressed. You have been running since this morning. It's six o'clock. Go run some bath water and take a nap. When we are done, we will lock the door. After all, it's your birthday. Why you trying to look run over by a truck?" said Imani.

"Thank you girlies," said Lillian. "I don't know where I would be without you guys."

Later, Lillian stepped out of bed and thought; *I didn't realize I was so tired. Time to get dressed. Splashing cold water to my face.* Lillian slowly started the process of getting dressed. She added moisturizer to her face and body, followed by golden and bronze tone eye shadow. Lillian fingered her hair with shine drops to loosen the pin curls, allowing her hair to fall naturally and frame her face. She stepped into white fitted capris with gold ankle strap stiletto heels paired with a goddess style gold and yellow halter top. The outfit showed off shapely legs and an ultra-feminine silhouette.

Emerging from her bedroom at nine, Lillian admired the job the girlies had done. The house decorations and entrance foyer reflected the golden time theme. Soft music played throughout the house, provided by the deejay. Everything was set up. Food drinks, and favors were all in place. The little ladies were dressed and ready. "Oh my god! Thank you ladies. Jared, where are my friends and why aren't you dressed?"

"They went to get dressed. Everything is done. Imani asked me to move the cake at about fifteen after. That way the cake can remain cool as long as possible. For your information, I am dressed. I have on khaki slacks with a white button down shirt. My shirt has a gold and bronze dragon on the back," said Jared.

"Hey ladies," said Lillian.

"Happy birthday girlie," they said in unison.

"I hope you enjoy your special day," said Imani.

"Thank you for setting up and finishing the food."

"No problem girlie, but next time you need to go with a restaurant. Girl you know we're getting too old to be working this hard," said Alexis.

Shaking her head and laughing at her friends, Lillian said, "You are correct, Alexis."

Jared leaned forward to accept another shrimp. Moving his date to the left, he slowly kissed her neck. Sitting in the living room on a white couch, he was whispering into his date's ear, "Girl you look too good tonight. Thank you for coming. Do you want to dance? The deejay is working it." Sliding his fingers across her legs, Jared moved her limbs onto his lap. "Where are my shrimp sexy?"

"Stop playing Jared. Where is your wife?"

"I don't know. I don't care. I'm doing what I want to do. I'm enjoying the company of an especially beautiful woman. Baby, you didn't answer my question."

"Look Jared, when you invited me here you didn't say this was your wife's birthday party. All of your families are here." His date seemed both scared and fed up at the same time.

"Sssh girl. No worries. Just keep feeding me my shrimp."

Lillian slowly walked through the room, offering everyone crawfish bruschetta.

"Jared, would you like a bruschetta?" *Oh my god, Jared is truly being an asshole tonight. Jesus, I need you to help pull this together. My mother is too upper class to witness foolishness at a party… besides she would only blame me. A good woman does anything needed to keep her husband happy and overlooks any negativity…*

"Sure, Lillian," said Jared. He turned to the woman sitting next to him. "Baby would you like a bruschetta?" Jared asked. She stood up to get off Jared's lap and stated, "No Jared I wouldn't like one," "Jared I'm going to be going now."

"No baby, don't leave stay, eat, and drink. We are going to have some fun tonight," he pleaded and begged with his woman.

Alexis took in the scene before her while hitting the other girls in the head. "Ladies mobilize, our friend needs us." Imani quickly pulled Jared by the hand and demanded, "Suga let's dance. Boy, you know that's my song." Imani led Jared away from his woman and the girls. Shannon grabbed Jared's woman by the arm and led her to the bathroom.

"Who comes to a house party to be the date for a married man?"

"Let go of my arm," said the woman as she pulled back.

"Don't let go ... push that trick in the bathroom, what kind of whore are you?" said Alexis.

"Look, I didn't come here for no trouble... I was just about to leave," said the woman. "Humph, the trick says, she didn't want any trouble. Biiitttcchh, please you thought you and Jared got our girl by the clit. Jared might be the shit to Lillian, but our girlie is the truth of that relationship," said Alexis.

"I'm perfectly able to use the restroom and refresh myself. As soon as I'm done, I will be leaving," said the woman. Shannon looked the woman from head to toe and asked, "Do you smell a rancid, sour, cheesy and out a place whore?"

"Now since you mentioned it, I do smell something putrid," said Candy. "Mirror, Mirror, on the wall, what should a Candy girl do to get rid of that smell?"

Grabbing the woman by the hair with a tight grip, Shannon pulled the woman into a running shower. "I don't know what the mirror says, but I say let's give the sour one a shower to wash away her sins and stench."

Alexis pulled the woman from the shower and wiped her face with a rag. "Girl, let me help you get refreshed. I don't know what came over my girlfriends." Alexis dried her hands on a bath towel and scanned the friends and woman in the bathroom. "Ladies, everyone important in the world to our friend is out there. So you know we can never let this trick go back in the party." Shannon looked to her right and then to Alexis. "What should we do?"

"Girl we are going to go old school!" Alexis said. Alexis reached into her purse and pulled out a tube of lipstick. Pulling the woman by the head, Alexis wrote an "A" for Adultery and "W" for whore on the woman's face. She then snatched the dress off the woman and wrote "H" for hoe on her back.

"Bitches, Stop!" said the woman. Clunk! Clunk! The woman started to fight. "What you think you can push on me and I not fight back?" said the woman. Pulling her arm from the ladies, she hit her head on the woman holding her arm and pushed the woman trying to write on her back into the shower wall. The woman yelled at the friends in the bathroom, "Leave me alone! You bitches just crazy. I told you I was leaving, he didn't say this was his wife's party." said the woman. "When I catch you bitches in the street, I got you," she said. The woman continued to hit and swing at the ladies in the bathroom.

Alexis leaned forward into the mirror, checking her reflection. "Do I see a red mark?" You need to get going before you get the real beat down. What self-respecting trick comes to her man's house with his wife to feed him shrimp?"

"Are you really trying to talk to this whore?" said Candy.

"I told you simple bitches, I didn't know his wife was going to be here."

A frown crept on- to Alexis's face as she noticed a slight bruise. She looked at the whore before her. "Bitch," said Alexis. The woman took in the scene before her and saw the opportunity for a quick getaway. She ran between the women and out the bathroom towards the back door away from the music. The woman frantically ran away from the party to her car. The girlies checked their appearances in the mirror before re-entering the party. Alexis moved her hair to hide her bruise from Lillian. "Ladies be cool, Lillian cannot know about the bathroom."

Imani continued to sway to the beat with her friend's husband. "Damn, negro you are truly a beast. How can you do you in front your shared family?"

Jared continued to dance with Imani and paused for a moment and replied, "Girl, I get my wife is your friend but, my business is my business."

After, an hour of dancing and continued eating, Lillian entered the cake tent for the happy birthday song to be sung. *When this party is over, I am going to plan my revenge on Jared. This Negro done lost his mind. Did he really just bring his whore into our home? Girl, stay focused and keep smiling. You don't need anyone to bring this up. Appearance and wealth are everything.* Releasing a quick burst of air, Lillian blew out all the candles at once. Imani quickly cut the cake and passed it out to party guests.

"Girlie everything was beautiful, but I'm going to get going. Enjoy the rest of your evening," said Shannon.

"Good night, Lillian," said Candy.

Wrapping her arms around Lillian's shoulders, Alexis said, "Girlie you didn't tell us you guys were swingers. Now that's some interesting conversation for our weekly Thursday night gatherings. You always in the spot talking and promoting black business, you need to tell us about your other men. I guess you do be promoting your husband. Damn girlie, you two got it going on," said Alexis.

Tapping Alexis on the shoulder, Imani said, "Stop that! Now you know you need to leave our friend alone."

"Good night ladies. Thanks again for everything."

Lillian rolled over in her bed to face her husband. "Good evening, Jared. How are you doing? Pulling back the sheet, she got up and walked towards the closet, then turned to face Jared. "Can I speak to you for a minute?" she asked.

"Sure Lillian, What's up?" said Jared.

"How is your woman? Is she the Negro on the phone that made you smile? I need you to respect my fucking mind. How is it you lay here, have daughters here, but you choose to eat shrimp and kiss another woman in my party? How is it you rub her face and play tapas at my party? When you were sick, I held your hand, held dick, and wiped your ass, but have I ever asked you to open up my pussy and help me use the bathroom?" Pushing Jared on the forehead, she said, "I have your girls and you would disrespect me in front of both our families. Now that's what's up. You will respect me in my house or you will be very sorry," Lillian screamed."That's what up! Did you see our mothers' faces? Did you see my parents? What about the neighbors? Jared did you see our friends staring at you?"

"Look it's no big deal," Jared replied. "Just shared a few shrimp with a friend. Look woman, I'm in no mood for your shit. Like I said before, you don't like something, you can leave." Crossing the room from the closet, Jared pulled the sheets back from the bed and turned off the light. "Good night Lillian," said Jared.

Candy

S *helby, momma needs a drink. My friend just was humiliated by her husband in front her whole world. Lillian must be destroyed, her husband playing in their living room with his other woman riding his lap. Two more lights and we will be at the club. Momma needs a drink and to dance.*

Candy parked the car, walked up the street in a fitted gold halter dress. She peeped her head through the hallway and waved at the deejay. Candy entered the room, smiling, and started to groove to the beat.

"A sweet girl has just entered the building and this King wants some Candy. All right people follow me, when I say we want Candy. What do I want?"

"We want Candy. I want Candy. I want you. Crowd... what we want? We want Candy," said King.

"Candy girl, this deejay thinks you look great," said King.

"Hello," said Candy.

"Hello back," said King.

"When did you learn my name?" replied Candy.

"A man meets a beautiful woman. She won't tell him her name. So man has to investigate. Sandals, you were too cute and sexy in that hammock. A brother had to work his show, find out your name and your haunts. I heard you came here on Sunday nights. You would be surprised to know how much you can find out about a person from a bartender," replied King.

"Well, King, I thank you for the mix or should I say remix," said Candy.

"You are quite welcome, Sandals," said King.

"Crown and seven my King," said Candy.

"Umm, I must have made an impression on the stunning lady because she just brought a drink for a deejay," said King.

Candy returned to the bar to scan the crowd in the club. "Excuse me bartender. Can you send the gentleman at the table with the blue light a drink for me?" said Candy.

"Sure, but lady, he is at that table with a woman," said the bartender.

"I see her, but he is hot." Candy kissed a napkin and passed it to the bartender to place under the drink. "Please send the gentleman a candied apple caramel swirl martini," said Candy.

"Oh, don't say who it's from. I will make it worth your time," said Candy.

Candy lounged on a barstool facing the outdoor patio. Her thoughts swirled around Lillian's birthday party. Caramel Crème and Nikki were sitting in the VIP section. Raising a martini glass to her lips, Candy slow sipped an apple martini.

In a quick glance on the way to the restroom, Candy spotted Justin's friends out having drinks. Stopping by the table and leaning forward to greet everyone with air kisses, she asked, "Where is my friend?"

"Hey Candy girl. Justin's at work tonight," said Marcus.

"Well gentlemen, you guys need to tell Justin to take some time off." Twirling around in a tight circle to allow all the men to gaze at her sexy appearance in the too tight dress, she said, "Marcus right?"

"Yeah my name is Marcus."

"Okay, Marcus, please remind Justin about what he is missing with all that work. If you were my man, would you let me come out in this dress alone?" said Candy.

"Umm, lady, I don't know. But you are wearing that dress," said Marcus.

"Good night men."

A chorus of men said "Goodnight" back.

"I've got to pee" said Candy as she entered the club's restroom. *Please don't let there be a line.* Stepping into the stall, Candy wiggled around to lift the dress and pull down her thong without ripping the tight dress.

Candy strolled to a mirror at the counter to wash her hands and check her makeup. Dusting her face with powder and reapplying lip-gloss, Candy stared at her awesome reflection.

She glanced in the mirror at the woman standing next to her.

"Hi," said Nikki. "We have so much in common."

"Excuse me do we know each other?"

"Why of course we know each other, you're the woman I saw running from my fiancé's house." Turning to the right, Nikki extended her hand to Candy. "How are you doing today? By the way my name is Nicole Charbonnet and Shane is my fiancé."

"Who is Shane?" Candy asked.

"Umm, now you don't know Shane. But didn't you just send him a drink from the bar?" said Nicole.

"Look, Nicole right? I don't know what you are talking about or who you are talking about. But, if your man is into me …consider him gone. Candy gets what and whom she wants." Candy continued to apply makeup and stare at the woman. "Miss … look at me and look at you. Do you really think any man would pick you?"

"You look. My wedding is in a few weeks, so consider yourself warned; leave Shane the fuck alone," said Nikki.

"Bitch, please. Shane is mine for as long as it moves me. Any w-h-o, you need to step your game and check your man. Remember I control the King in this chess game. Back off miss," said Candy.

"Like I said, leave my husband alone," said Nicole.

Candy gave the woman an intense stare with a strong dismissal. Candy twisted her face, flicked her hair over her shoulder, and replied, "Husband? Now I know you are confused, you don't get a husband until after the ceremony, until then, all is fair in love and war."

Stepping out of the restroom, glancing left and right, Candy checked all around for girlfriend backup. *Damn, I'm alone and Nicole is here trying to flex. But, she needs to know Caramel Crème is for me and not her. After all, I will have a little crème soon with any luck.*

Candy sat behind the wheel of her car and pulled her cell phone from her purse. Quickly she dialed Shannon's number. "I need you girlie! Where are you?"

"I'm at the condo and this is not a good time. I just got in here from Lillian's party and Derrick will lose his mind if I leave out again. Girl do you know what time it is?" said Shannon.

"Yes, I know but I have problems," said Candy.

"Candy you know the rules, just chill. I will call you first thing in the morning," replied Shannon.

"What's up with you?" answered Candy.

"Nothing is up, Candy, but Derrick is jealous at times. Me going out after getting a phone call would not be good," replied Shannon.

"Okay, Shannon," said Candy.

"Later."

Alexis

An hour later, Alexis parked in front of Michael's door and ran to ring the bell. Pressing the bell three times, Alexis slowly blew out a breath and waited for the door to open. Mike peeped at Alexis at the door and wondered what happened at the party to bring her across the river in the middle of the night. "Mom, I need to go. Alexis is ringing the doorbell," said Michael.

"Okay, son," she replied. "But have you told her yet?"

"Don't start that talk. I'm enjoying dating and spoiling Alexis. I want to enjoy her as long as possible," replied Michael. "Good night, Mom"

"Goodnight baby...but know I worry about you," she said.

Leaning on the doorbell, Alexis placed her head on the wall and continued to wait for Michael to answer the door. *Okay, Michael what's up? You never take this long to answer the door.*

Michael moved from his window seat, walked to the door, and opened it for Alexis's entry.

"Hey baby. Come in," replied Michael as he moved to allow Alexis to enter.

"Hi Suga," said Alexis. She pushed the door closed and jumped into Michael's arms. Wrapping her legs around his back, Alexis kissed every inch of Suga's face. "Baby, I missed you."

"Alexis is everything all right with you?" said Michael.

"Yes," replied Alexis.

"Alexis you almost knocked a brother down, jumping in my arms. How was Lillian's birthday bash? I didn't expect you to come over tonight," said Michael.

Answering Michael's questions with more and more kisses, Alexis slid down his body to touch the floor. "Suga, the food was excellent, the decorations were golden in tone, and theme, the deejay was great. But the party, was out of control," said Alexis.

"Well, woman, sounds like a good time was had by all," said Michael.

Alexis quickly walked deeper into the house and joined Michael on an oversized chair. She kissed his face from ear to ear. "Suga the party was interesting. Lillian's husband completely embarrassed her in front of all of us. Her parents and his parents were at the party. Half the city was at the party. Suga, Jared had this heifer riding his lap and feeding him shrimp throughout the party. It was horrible. My girl was walking around offering appetizers to guests while her husband was sitting on the couch letting a bitch feed him. For once, Candy and I agreed on what needed to happen. I thought we should play baseball and take turns swinging at his head. But, Shannon and Imani felt we should just ignore it and let our friend have her special day. But in the end, we took his trick to the bathroom and gave her a bath to get rid of her smell. I don't know what or how to describe the party, Suga."

Gulping the last of his drink, Michael moved Alexis from his lap and went to pour a drink for the both of them. Offering her a glass, he said, "Here, you need something to sip. Is this why you didn't want me to come to the party?"

"Suga, nobody in my circle knows I'm seeing you or anyone for that matter. When we go out Candy and Shannon are always bragging on the brothers they date. I just want to keep you and me private. I love the way you treat me. I'm afraid of letting others enter into our private world. At this time, nobody knows about us so nobody can try and steal our joy," said Alexis.

He twirled her hair between his fingers, then quietly whispered into her ear, "It's okay for now beautiful. But, Alexis we are only going to remain a secret for a while. I love you," said Michael.

Every muscle in Alexis' body tightened with the mention of love.

Michael leaned Alexis' head forward so their eyes were in a straight line. "Baby, I love you."

Alexis took in a deep gulp of air and told Suga, "I love you too, baby."

Michael smiled at Alexis and lifted her in his arms. He carried her to his bedroom, and whispered into Alexis' ear, "What did you enjoy most about the party?"

"Umm, just hanging out with my friends. The party was cool for the most part. It was just the dance floor and surrounding area that was too hot for comfort," said Alexis.

Michael quickly lay down across the bed, fitting Alexis inside his arms. Slowly he traced her body with his eyes while removing her party clothes. Dropping the clothes to the floor, Michael pulled a cover over their intertwined bodies.

Alexis silently said a prayer in the curve of Suga's arm and closed her eyes. *One, two, three, four, girl you got to calm down. This man is a dream. Jesus please don't let this be a bad dream. He is too good to be true and it will hurt too much if this is faux. He really wants me, Alexis. Lawd have mercy.* "Good night Suga," said Alexis.

"Good night Alexis," said Michael.

"Baby you are too good to me. I just love our dealings and us," said Alexis.

"Alexis you need to stop thinking about us and enjoy us. Baby I'm not a client. We are very good together. Now beautiful, we need to get some rest. Ssh...Baby let's go to sleep."

"Where the fuck have you been?" an angry voice screamed throughout the condo.

Walking deeper into the condo, Shannon said, "Derrick, can you calm down? You are well aware that tonight was Lillian's birthday party. Remember I mentioned the "golden time" party last week. After all, your ass was well aware I had to set up decorations and food for the event. If it was all that, why didn't you come to the party?"

"I don't intend to spend time with the bitches you hang in the street with," said Derrick.

"Look, don't talk about my friends. Lillian is not having a good night. Lillian's party was a mess. Her husband is out of his mind."

"I don't want to hear about you and your friends or your friend's husbands."

"Derrick, I need to leave out. Candy is upset. Lillian is upset. I need to go help my friends." She picked up the phone.

"What? You need to go take a shower and come to bed," he demanded.

"Derrick… Lillian is my friend."

"So, fucking what?" yelled Derrick. "Does she have a husband?"

"Yes," said Shannon.

"Do you have a husband?" asked Derrick through closed teeth.

"No," replied Shannon.

"Do you want to have a husband and a condo downtown?" asked Derrick.

"Derrick, I love you," said Shannon. "Why are you acting fucking crazy? When we started dating, we'd go for runs and jog all over. We would go out to eat and just have fun. Baby what's wrong?" said Shannon.

"Nothing is wrong," said Derrick.

Placing the phone back on its charger, Shannon turned to face Derrick. "Baby what is wrong?"

Smack, punch! Derrick's hands connected with Shannon's torso as he punched her. "Bitch, are you fucking crazy? You come in from a party that I didn't want you to go to and then your ass is trying to leave out?"

Rolling into a ball to protect her face and body from blows, Shannon screamed for Derrick to stop. "Stop! Stop! Derrick, I can't believe you are hitting on me." As she pushed forward to slap Derrick in the face, he yelled, "Bitch you are not going to hurt me."

Derrick's body tightened at the nerve of Shannon trying to fight back. Pushing her hard into the wall, Derrick turned to go upstairs.

Shannon shut her eyes and slid down the wall to the floor. *Damn! He hit me into the wall.* Shannon screamed at Derrick while jumping to her feet. "Bitch! How could you hit me?" Shannon went to the kitchen, grabbed a stainless steel skillet, and ran upstairs two steps at time. Diving into bed, she connected with the left side of Derrick's face.

"Bitch ass Negro, you hit me," said Shannon.

Shannon covered Derrick's body, hitting him three times with the skillet. Shannon screamed at the top of her lungs, "Bitch! You asshole! I just went to a girlfriend's party and you act like I screwed another man in your face. I be damn if your ass is going to hit on me and I not hit back. You are a sorry ass man."

"Shannon! Get off me now before I really knock you out!"

"Whatever, Bitch," said Shannon.

"Get off me," said Derrick.

She slammed the skillet into his body, over and over, followed by punches to his groin and ribs.

Derrick tightened his jaw as he bit down, matching up his teeth, grabbing Shannon by her arms, and rolling on top of her body. "Shannon, stop Look, I'm sorry, I hit you. Must you be so damn drastic? Look, I am going to stop. Can you calm down?"

"Yeah, Derrick. I can calm down when you get your hands off me. Do you feel my hands caressing the dick? If you don't stop, I will play twister with the dick. Get the fuck off me bitch."

"All right, Shannon. I will let go of your arms when you let go of my dick."

"Sure, you first," said Shannon. She jumped up, grabbed a suitcase from the closet, and threw it on the bed.

"Shannon, hold up, girl. I'm sorry. Why are you packing a bag to leave?"

Shannon turned and stared at Derrick. "Bitch, I'm not leaving you are. After all, I'm a female that you just beat up on and slammed into the wall. When I call the police, can you imagine what they will say? Derrick I'm holding the phone, you have three minutes to get out and not return. I will call the police and fake an active attack." Looking at the phone, she pressed 9-1- ."Baby, wait! Don't do that dumb shit," said Derrick.

"What dumb shit Derrick? You mean letting a man beat the hell out of me for spending some time with my girlfriends?" Shannon continued to watch Derrick, who stumbled while trying to put on his pants. Shannon threw an overnight bag to Derrick while escorting him to the door. "Bye, Derrick... don't come back here."

"Baby! Why you tripping?" said Derrick.

"Good night, Derrick. Do you want me to call that last 1 and start some drama?"

"Bye, Shannon."

Moments later, outside the condo, Derrick was stopped by a police officer.

"Excuse me, sir, can we see your hands? Did you just leave condo 4083? There were several calls to the police about raised voices and sounds of a struggle."

"Yes officer. I just left that apartment. Me and my lady friend just had a difference of opinion," said Derrick.

"Okay, sir, your name please?"

"My name is Derrick."

"Well, Derrick, we are going to talk to your lady friend and get to the bottom of this."

Bam! Bam! Bam! "It's the police please open the door!"

Shannon turned, locked the door, set the alarm system to the condo, and grabbed the phone. She placed it on the bed, then she texted Candy and Alexis. "Girlie down, Condo. Help me!" *Damn the police are here. Oh well he hit me first.* Pressing in the deactivation code, Shannon slowly opened the door for the police. "Can I help you officers?"

"Is there a problem here ma'am?"

"No problem officers, just a heated debate between two people. Derrick was just leaving and I was headed to bed," said Shannon.

"Ma'am, have you seen your face? Can you tell us how that happened?"

"Oh officers I fell down when running upstairs," said Shannon.

"Ma'am we need you to step out the condo and come with us."

Lillian

mani turned left to stretch her back and legs before beginning the suicide stroll.

"Hi Lillian," said Imani.

"Hey girlie, you started stretching," said Lillian.

"Yep. You know I am afraid of the suicide stroll but will always show up and out for a friend," said Imani.

"Thank you girl. Where is everybody else?" said Lillian.

Imani turned to face her friend and answered, "Alexis is sitting in the car on the phone. Candy and Shannon started to jog in place down by the bench at the foot of the bridge."

Alexis slipped her bag from her shoulder and placed her car keys in the pocket of her jogging suit. Blowing out a breath while touching her toes, she said, "Hey, girlies, how you feeling?"

Lillian turned and smiled at Alexis. "I'm good friend."

Lillian, Alexis, and Imani slowly started the suicide stroll, trying to play catch up with Candy and Shannon.

"Hey, I called this extra suicide stroll to try and figure out what to do next. How those girlies done left us and started running without all the friends? Thank you ladies for making my birthday a success. My golden time party was so beautiful. I will remember your efforts for the rest of my life. But Jared ....Now that bitch ass Negro made me want to jump through the ceiling and come back to earth landing on his dick. Did you girlies see him flossing with a heffa on his lap at my birthday party? I told him I'm what's up in our house. Ladies, my daughters saw him with another woman. My baby keeps asking, *Mommy is everything okay? Who was that woman with Daddy?* Just what exactly do I say to my child?" asked Lillian to her friends.

"Well, Lillian, don't beat yourself up. Tell your girls the truth," said Alexis.

"What? I can't tell my girls the truth," she replied.

"Sure you can. Tell them you don't know who the woman was and ask them to ask their Dad. After all, you both are parents and you both are responsible for helping them feel safe and secure," said Imani.

"Now, my two mental health professional friends have lost their damn minds," said Lillian.

"Well, why do you have to be the heavy here? He did the dirt right?" said Alexis.

"Yeah he did the dirt but I don't want to hurt my girls," replied Lillian as they continued to walk along the lake.

"At this point it's about you. Children are resilient ... they can bounce back from anything. You just make sure you are personally okay with everything going on now. Friend that was a very shocking display. I don't think

I could have handled that situation so gracefully. How can Jared act like that in front of your parents and his parents?" said Imani.

"Girl, I don't know, but I do know I want to get my walk on and just breathe for a minute," said Lillian.

"Where are the girls?" said Imani.

"Oh, girlies, my mom is keeping them to give me a minute to think, process, and figure out what's next," said Lillian.

"Imani, are you and Lillian ready to join us in a nice suicide run on the lake?" said Candy.

"Nope, ladies ... you know I'm afraid of this walk, let alone trying to run out here. Besides we came to listen to our friend not run a marathon," replied Imani.

"Well, hello ladies. Let's enjoy a nice peaceful walk while watching a lively lake in the background," said Lillian.

Lillian slowed down, bent over, and pulled in a short breath. "Ladies, must we walk this fast?"

"Yes, we are trying to get into new sizes. We are walking to get some mental clarity but obtaining a new size is extra added benefit," said Candy.

"Girl I swear ... must you always be focused on the size of your ass?" said Lillian.

"Yep. You know I'm trying to land that King Orca to pay my bills and put me up in a condo downtown with multiple credit cards. You know I'm trying to get on that Shannon plan and work my show to new cars and letters on my name," replied Candy.

"Anyway ladies, let's meet at Shannon's condo for drinks and appetizers," said Lillian.

Shannon turned and faced the friends. "Ladies, I don't know about drinks at my place. Last night was not a good evening between Derrick and me. He was acting like he lost his mind when I got in."

"Yesterday must have been a full moon," said Candy.

"What the hell, let's party? After we walk, we eat. Derrick can't bother me and his shitty ass moods," said Shannon.

Plopping down on the red sofa at her condo, Shannon filled the last available spot. "Well ladies, I just ordered some pizza. In the meantime, we have some shrimp dip with pita chips, spicy chipotle wings, chips, and all the liquor we can possibly drink. You know Derrick loves me, my pussy, and expensive liquors from around the world. Last night he hit my shit list so tonight we drink his shit to get even," said Shannon.

"Hey, friend, are you sure about this? You and King Orca were hot and heavy last night. Girlie, you did send out a "GD" text with special instructions?" said Candy.

"Look Candy, Derrick was out of his mind. This is our condo and who says I can't have my friends over?" replied Shannon.

"Shannon, what's up? If we shouldn't be here, then say it so we can leave before there is any drama," said Imani.

Shannon stopped and looked over her shoulder to Imani. "Hold it together and stop worrying."

"I'm not worrying, Shannon. I just think you should avoid conflict wherever possible. After all, you and this man share a home and an intimate relationship," said Imani.

"All I know is Derrick bet not come here. Besides, I've moved my important papers to my Moms. My time here with Derrick is ending. I have truly enjoyed the trips, food, shopping, and this place. But his constant feeling I'm cheating on him is really too much for me. He needs to be more confident in our relationship and the way I treat him."

"Shannon, be for real, look at how you met him and how quickly you guys moved in together? Did you really think there would be no problems?" said Lillian.

"Lillian, every man is not your husband. Speak for your damn self ... just cause Jared is fucking over you, you don't need to become bitter and critical of every man in America," said Shannon.

"Bitch, who exactly are you calling bitter? At least I'm not fucking every man that shows me a little attention," replied Lillian.

"Well, the way Jared has fucked over, under, and stepped on your ass for the last few years, you should have beaten me to quite a few men," answered Shannon.

"Girlies, can we stop it and remember we are friends," said Imani.

"Nah, no girl. Let them be. We are finally starting to have some good ole conversing about men and relationships. I have been waiting on this moment for a minute. After all, we all have seen Jared act out and heard stories of the power of the pussy," said Alexis.

"Look, it's looking like we can't have a sip of wine, let alone sit down in this nice condo and relax for the evening," said Imani.

"Look, I wish Derrick would bring his crazy, jealous, trying to confront somebody's ass in here. I'm ready. I'm always carrying a nice knife and am willing to play darts in his ass if needed," said Alexis.

"Girlies, can we have a toast?" asked Imani as she poured drinks for the friends.

"A toast?" said Shannon.

"Yes," replied Imani. "We need to change the energy and move towards relaxing and peace."

The door opened and Derrick walked in.

"Shannon. Shannon. Shannon. Why the fuck all these bitches in my house drinking my liquor and eating my food?" said Derrick.

"Derrick, this is my house too, and these are my friends," said Shannon. "I would appreciate it if you don't talk to them in that tone or with the language you just used," replied Shannon.

"Once again, who the fuck do you think you're talking to? I run everything in here and you need to get the fuck out and take your bitches with you," said Derrick.

"Hi to you too, asshole," said Alexis.

Shannon grabbed the phone from its cradle and pressed 9-1.

"Derrick, I thought we came to an agreement last night. You get out and I won't call the police ... but you leave a girlie no choice. I am about to fake a call, have a friend hit me in the face, and blame it all on you, because I've tried to be fair and share space and time, but you are greedy and want everything for you. Well, I'm greedy too. I want to enjoy the condo with my friends without being harassed. Since, my name is on the lease, please get the fuck out, and don't come back. Good night with your bitch ass self," said Shannon.

"Bye, Derrick," said the girlies.

"Bye, Derrick," said Shannon.

"All right, Shannon, I'm leaving. Remember you won't always have the phone to save your ass. This house is for me and my relations with women." Derrick grabbed his iPod, turned, and left out the condo.

"Well that's over. Girlies please raise your glasses. I propose a toast to garbage leaving and enjoying a beautiful night," said Shannon. "Thank you ladies for coming get me out of jail.".

"That's a toast, but a better one is, Here's to getting a restraining order," said Alexis. Clink, clink. A chorus of friends all said "Restraining order."

Caramel Crème

K nock, Knock, knock. "Where the hell are you, Candy? Open the damn door and let me in. Candy. Candy. That's all right ...be like this. I will just sit down and wait for you to open this door. If you are not home, at some point you have to come home," said Shane.

Ring, Ring, Ring.

"Hello" said Shane, answering his phone as he sat in his car.

"Shane, where are you? Baby you're not home. I just left my parents ... we were talking about our marriage and your upcoming run for office," Nikki said.

"Nikki, look. I'm out with the fellas having a few beers, and now is not a good time," replied Shane.

"Which bar? It is mighty quiet. What? Y'all the only people in there, or something?" asked Nicole.

"No. I just stepped outside to take this call when I saw it was you," replied Shane.

"What?" Blowing a frustrated breath into the phone, she said, "What ... you can't talk to me in front your precious ass friends?" asked Nicole. "I'm so sick of the secrets and you hiding my calls."

"Ssh, baby sssh. I'm not hiding your calls. I was just trying to be polite and respectful. But, I will most definitely take your future calls in the bar," said Shane.

"Shane, baby, what bar are you at?" asked Nicole.

"Why, Nikki?" said Shane.

"Well, maybe a few of my friends and I can meet you and your friends," said Nicole.

"Nikki, now is not a good time. We are in a conference," said Shane.

"Shane baby. I love you and I want us to be a success. If you have secrets, sweetie, and are planning a political career, we are never going to make it. My parents and I were discussing our rise to power, and baby, you don't have any major skeletons? Right?" said Nicole.

"Nikki, get off the phone. I'm not going to talk with you and ignore my friends. Bye," said Shane.

"Stop it. Stop all the damn lies. I know your ass is not at no bar with some friends. My friends told me they saw you in the street with some red bitch. I am so sick of you, your lies, and this upcoming wedding. You are always trying to put me in a box. Well, put me in all your plans box or stop calling me all together. Shane, do you hear me?" said Nicole.

Shane tightened his grip on the phone. "I hear you. Bye," said Shane.

Pick up, pick up, and answer the phone.

Candy reached into her purple Furla hobo bag and grabbed the phone. "Hello," said Candy.

"What's up sexy? Where you at? This is my tenth call to you. Where you at?"

"I'm in my skin. Where is your fiancé at?" said Candy. "Caramel Crème I thought we agreed to slow this thing down. You are about to get married and I'm tired of pretending I'm cool with our situation. I want more than a quick hit when your wifey is out with her moms. Is that all I'm good for?" said Candy.

"Candy girl why are you tripping? I'm sitting at your house now, trying to give you time," said Shane.

"Well you didn't call or say you were coming. I have friends, a job, and have been trying to find my own king. After all, you about to become somebody else's king on a full time basis," said Candy.

"Once again Candy, why are you tripping? We have been getting down for over a year with no problems. Now, when I'm sitting at your door wanting to spend time with you, why are you acting like we are strangers?" said Caramel Crème.

"Mr. Crème, I'm walking up the steps to my apartment now. If your bitch ass is not on my steps, I'm going to hop back in Shelby, roll up to your house, and kick that ass," said Candy.

"Ha. Ha. Like you can really kick my ass?" said Caramel Crème.

"Is that a threat?" asked Candy as she walked to the top of the steps.

"Yep, and I will make it a promise. Besides, it will be the moment to define all moments in our friendship," said Caramel Crème.

Candy dragged up the steps, one at a time after a night of drinks at Shannon's place. "Caramel Crème, tonight has been shitty from start to finish. I'm not in the mood for any more Negroes thinking they can walk on a female. Shannon got a bitch ass Negro with a few dollars and a serious need to get knocked the fuck out, and, well, I need to call a few friends from back in the day to knock out Jared."

Candy entered the house kicking off tennis while pulling her black, white, and fuchsia exercise tank overhead and pulling the pants from her body. "Come on in Caramel Crème …just getting home from a suicide stroll and drinks." Dropping the workout clothes in the hamper, Candy entered the bathroom and turned on the shower. Stepping in front the mirror to admire her curvy figure and luscious breasts, Candy invited Crème to the shower. *Mirror. Mirror. I don't know how the Negro could possibly want anybody else. Just look at me. I am fine, smart, and super sexy. When I step in any spot, everyone just wishes they could sex me and the bitches just get mad because I steal their attention. How could he ever think he could mess over me with a fiancée? Who cares if she was first? In the end, I will be the only one. If that means no political career... oh well. Candy gets what Candy wants. I want you, Mr. Crème.*

"Caramel Crème, don't you want to come join me?" said Candy.

"Sure Candy. I'll join you and then will you join me in your bed?" said Caramel Crème.

"Crème please, you know we don't do that anymore …we can hit it on the sofa and have some fun," said Candy.

Candy reached down and grabbed Colossal's mushroom shaped head. "How are you today?" Pulling Caramel

Crème deeper into the shower Candy kissed Colossal hello. "I just loved doing that. Too bad it won't be receiving hello much longer," said Candy.

"Candy, are you going to enjoy the dick or just pick fights with it? To me, under the nice warm water I'd rather embrace getting our fuck on," said Caramel Crème.

Candy stepped from under the warm shower spray to face Caramel Crème. "Mr. Crème, I stay ready to play… it's just you don't stay ready with your future wifey in your shadows," said Candy.

Pushing the shower curtain back, Crème grabbed Candy by the waist and pulled her back into shower. "Now, can we shower and enjoy each other?"

Leaning forward to give Crème a kiss, she said, "We will shower now and enjoy each other."

Thursday

S hannon scanned the table, making eye contact with all the friends, then asked, "Girlies, did you see the word of the week at Private Joy coffee shop?"

"Yes," said Imani. "We are the perfect example of the word. I don't know a greater example than us?"

"Private Joy's word of the week was Friendship; the state of being attached to another person by affection, esteem, or emotions; to favor another person and make choices based on another's feelings," said Lillian.

"Well, Lillian, can you think of another example of the word friendship?"

"Before last week, I would have said Jared and me," replied Lillian.

"Bitch, be real. You would have said you and Jared were examples of friendship?" said Alexis.

"Yes Alexis. Jared and I have been friends for years. He is everything to me. I still find it so hard to believe he would bring another woman into our home and disrespect me in front of our girls. After all, we have been together for years and built a family," said Lillian.

"Ladies, can we order some drinks? I am overdue for a few drinks. Our Thursday night outings are a part of my mental health refresher after listening to too many problems. I am tired of problems and would like to focus on fun," said Alexis.

"Well I agree with you ... let's order some drinks," said Imani.

"Candy, Candy, what are you drinking tonight? You are the only friend who has not told Joe what you are having," said Alexis.

"I'm good ladies... I'll have something simple ... a crown and seven, light ice please," replied Candy.

"Candy that's a different drink for you," said Imani. "You normally get martinis and vodka based drinks."

Candy covered her mouth to hide a slight yawn. "Umm, ladies. I have been a little tired and need to make another stop before heading in tonight."

"What's up with you?" said Shannon.

"Girl, just need to make a run and check in on a potential sponsor," said Candy. "King is working a club tonight and I want to check him out on the tables."

"Um some better table dish. I was scared for a minute that girls' night out was going to turn into an extension of our jobs," said Alexis.

Imani leaned back in her chair while listening to Alexis and Candy move through their drama.

A few minutes later Imani jumped into chatter and asked, "Ladies did you have fun at the Panther's Palace or what? I want to go back and check out the club owner's show. Ladies, I used to love watching him pull it out and flip it left to right over a grill. Black Panther's penis is so beautiful. Have you girlies noticed the smooth skin leading up to the prettiest shiny little black hairs? How can even his dick hair be pretty?" said Imani.

Alexis laughed, "Girl do you hear yourself? Did you just describe his dick hair as being pretty?"

Taking a sip from her Jack and ginger ale, Imani turned to face Alexis. "Yes, I enjoy watching him and his beautiful penis."

"Girl, please stop it. You need to focus on something other than a man's penis. What about friendship, caring for another's feelings, and sharing a life?" said Lillian.

Imani turned and scanned the table to witness a collection of twisted sour faces. Slowly taking a sip of her spirits, she leaned forward to address Lillian. "Girl, look. I love you and our friendship but we were at the party and saw your husband with our own individual eyes. Can you take a slow sip of spirits and chill out?" said Imani.

"What? It's pick on Lillian day at Snug's?"

"No, it's not," said Alexis. "Lillian you need to be real and look into the light. Me, myself, and I come out on Thursdays to enjoy my friends and our friendship. I do not come out to enter into an alternate reality," said Alexis.

Placing a hand to her mouth to cover a yawn, Candy laughed at Lillian. Sipping another quick sip of crown and seven, she said, "Friend what do you want?"

"I want a husband and friends who respect me," said Lillian. Lillian sipped another bit of Remy and looked her friends in the eye. "Ladies, thank you for making my party a success and allowing me to vent all my frustrations. I love Jared and our life so much. I don't know what I will do if we can't weather this storm. Ladies, I don't want to be single raising my girls," said Lillian.

Silence beat back all the conversation at the table and all eyes focused in on Lillian. "Lillian, sweetie. We all love you and hold your friendship in high regard but, hear me as I say this … you need to find yourself again. What does Lillian want and desire outside of Jared? Girlie, do you remember you before the kids and husband? Cause I want you to know I do," said Alexis. "Ladies do the rest of you remember?"

"Well, for one, I do," said Imani, picking up the glass from the table and tapping glass to glass. "Let's toast to friendship and the rest of our evening."

Clink, Clink, Clink.

Imani

"Good morning, Trenell. How are things at Counseling Connections this morning?" said Imani.

"Well, everything is great. The interns and Alexis are hard at work with clients," replied Trenell. She picked up the coffee cup from the desk and looked over her morning coffee to address Imani. "Before you move another step you need to get Ms. Bossy out the waiting room. Oh my God. I know why she is here. Can you answer one question for me?" said Trenell.

"Yes Trenell," said Imani.

"When are you going to terminate with Shay?"

"Okay, Trenell I hear you, but can you get back to your office and let me handle my office?" said Imani.

Shay sat in lobby of Counseling Connections texting directions to everyone ...from her man, employees, and friends. Stomping to the receptionist's desk, she said, "Trenell, when is Ms. Flowers going to see me?"

Trenell quickly placed a finger to her lips and mouthed, "One moment, Ms. Waters, the counselor will be with you in a moment. This is an office waiting area for the counselors. Maybe you can bring a book or something for your future visits," said Trenell.

"Look I'm tired of waiting on Ms. Flowers. Why can't she see me now? After all, I'm here and I don't see but three other people in the waiting room," said Shay.

"Excuse me Ms. Waters. I must ask you to have a seat and be quiet. This office is a professional counseling center where all clients and appointments are respected," said Trenell.

Turning to face a collection of chairs, Shay grabbed a magazine from the table to wait on Ms. Flowers. "Humph. Why can't she ever be early on appointments?" said Shay.

"Ms. Waters, Imani will see you now," said Trenell.

"Hello Shay. How are you feeling today?" asked Imani.

"I'm feeling okay. I was just waiting out there forever to start my appointment. It would be novel if my appointment could start when I get here," said Shay.

Sitting down in an oversized chair facing Shay, Imani said, "I'm sorry for your annoyance but if you came for your scheduled time and not early you would not have those problems." Imani grabbed her water from the table and took a sip before proceeding with the session. "You have your fifty minutes now. What seems to be the problem today, Shay?"

"Well I've been coming here for months but I'm not making any progress with my husband. He never touches me anymore; he grills meat at all times of the morning. I even heard one of the neighbors ask him about it. He just eats, eats, and eats more food. The only other thing he does is play the devilish Xbox and Wii.

When I tell him what to do, he does it but he doesn't treat me the same anymore. For example, the other day I told him to cut the grass, make groceries, cook some chicken and yellow rice for us, wash the towels, change our sheets, and run me some bath water. Do you believe he wouldn't even listen to me when I got home? I mean I work so hard all day and he does nothing, and then he won't even express any concern for me. Can you believe his behavior?" said Shay.

"Well Shay, people come to counseling to discuss their feelings and discover ways they can change themselves. Counseling is not a magical place where you find a way to manipulate others," said Imani.

"Everyone down at the shop talks about coming here and learning so much about their relationships. Why not me?" said Shay.

Imani looked up from her notes and asked, "Are they learning about their relationships or are they learning about themselves? Shay what is it you want to achieve from coming here every week?" said Imani.

Shay exhaled a short breath. "I keep telling you I want to learn more about me and my husband and how to make us work. At the very least I want him to touch me."

"Have you asked him why he doesn't touch you anymore?" said Imani.

"No!" replied Shay with a raised voice. "I'm not going to ask him that. He is supposed to touch me. I'm his wife. I just know he better not be touching someone else. I want kids, and my sexy man back. I enjoyed walking in rooms and being the envy of every woman there. Now, I'm like everyone else that has a fat husband with no kids. I have nothing to show. I loved being chased and chosen. I mean… when I met my husband he was running with at least five women, maybe more, but he chose me."

Looking up from the notepad, Imani asked, "What's important about the number of women he ran with, and him choosing you?"

Shaking her head from left to right, Shay said, "Nothing. I'm just telling you about our experience."

"I don't think that's honest. His selection of you comes up in every session … along with you being envied by other women," said Imani.

Shay looked Imani in the eye and spoke. "I enjoy people watching me. I like to be superior to others and get my way. Now that we are married, I'm not getting my way and I'm no longer the envy of other women. I don't like that. I like to watch other people look at me in adoration. Him looking like Mr. Piggy does not get me the attention I want and desire."

"Shay, tell me more about your feelings for your husband," replied Imani.

Shay smiled and replied, "I love him."

"Do you love him or do you live for the attention he garners for you?" said Imani.

"I love the attention. He is nice too. Now he no longer does the things he did before we wed. If I can't have the super sexy man then, I should have two adorable kids that can gain me positive attention," said Shay.

"Before your husband, did you get all the attention you wanted?" asked Imani.

"Of course, don't be silly. Everywhere I go, people stare at me. Just look at me. I'm gorgeous, with slight curves. I make money. I boss everyone and control everything in my world." said Shay.

Lowering her pen to the pad Imani asked, "Does a man want a boss or a lover?"

"Well my husband knew who I was when he picked me," replied Shay with a twisted face.

"Be honest Shay. Don't try to hide behind your image. What does a man want?" said Imani.

"He wants someone who makes six figures and can make life easy for him," said Shay.

"What does a man want?" said Imani.

"He wants to live well," said Shay.

"Don't play pussy here, Shay. What does a man want?" Picking the pen up to add to her notes, Imani focused in on Shay. "Shay a man wants…Answer me, Shay. A man wants a what?"

"I don't know," said Shay.

Pulling the chair to sit directly in front of Shay, Imani said, "Bullshit! You know what a man wants. Are you willing to give your husband what he wants? It appears to me that he won't give you what you want until you give him what he wants. Do you think this man is unaware of what you want and enjoy?"

"I don't know. He doesn't touch me anymore and all he does is eat and play video games," replied Shay.

"Is that normal behavior for a grown man with skills and ability?" said Imani.

Shrugging her shoulders, Shay answered, "I don't know."

"How is he as a man? When was the last time you asked him about him and his day, not just his list of duties? Does this man work? Did he finish college? Shay what about you encourages you to treat humans the way you do?" said Imani.

"What do you mean? I don't understand," said Shay.

"Yes you do," Imani expressed.

"People are business and business is dealt with in a certain manner," said Shay.

"Ms. Waters, don't be silly here …can you answer that question honestly without all the bull, you like being in control?"

"Being in control makes me feel comfortable.

Imani continued to lean forward to Shay. "Are you getting your desired results from your behavior?"

"No," replied Shay.

"Have you considered doing something different?" said Imani.

"No."

"Ms. Waters, that is your time. You can make an appointment with the receptionist for next week or maybe two weeks. In the meantime, maybe you will give some thought to doing things differently in your home life and see what that will bring to you. Counseling interventions only work if the person in counseling is willing to change themselves. You should mentally review the things we have talked about in the counseling process," said Imani.

Shay left the office without making a reply.

Imani hurried home to change for her outing with David. Anthony had truly worked magic as a friend. He had introduced her to a new man. *Maybe, this brother won't have a mommie manager.*

Placing a hand on her shoulders, David turned Imani to face him. "Thanks," David said. "I was looking forward to continuing our conversations over drinks. Maybe we can even grab some dinner later. What you drinking?"

Imani continued to stare at the beautiful man, and replied, "Just a Louisiana Lemonade."

"What's that?" said David.

"Some lemonade mix, sour mix, New Orleans rum, and a splash of sprite poured over ice," said Imani.

"Well sir, thanks for the invite. It's not every day a girlie gets asked out by a handsome man with no baggage. I'm still shocked you asked me out," said Imani.

"Well I figured a drink at Snug's was cool. After all, you come here every Thursday with your friends," said David.

"That's true. But today is not Thursday and I'm not here with my girlies," said Imani.

"What you drinking?" asked Imani.

"Can I get you a drink sir?" the bartender asked.

"Crown and seven," replied David.

"How was your day?" asked Imani.

"My day has just improved by a million points. I have been looking forward to us getting together all afternoon. I'm tired of everyone and their drama at my practice," said David.

Imani pursed her lips to form the question, "What? The divorce attorney doesn't like drama. Oh my god! I'm about to go in shock. I thought you lived and breathed for drama and cheating on both sides."

"Well, some days I just want to be David and enjoy life," said David.

Imani smiled at David and raised her glass to his. Clink. "To good days with no drama and no problems." Imani and David both placed their drinks on the bar.

"Imani, I didn't get a chance to eat today at all, do you mind if we grab some dinner next door?" said David.

"I hadn't really planned it but, it's cool. Are you sure you want to share a meal?" said Imani.

"Positive. I'm not afraid to eat are you?" said David

A slow smile formed on her face. "No."

Touching her barstool, David slid it back from the bar. Grabbing her drink from the bar, he said, "This way me lady."

They shared a laugh as they walked into Snug's dining room.

"Is this table good with you or would you prefer the window?" said David.

"I would just adore the window," said Imani.

"Cool, the window it is," replied David. Placing the drinks on the table, he said, "Now how was your day, lady?"

Imani smiled at her dining companion. "The same as yours, long and filled with drama."

Imani smiled at the waitress as she approached the table. The waitress lit the single candle on the table as she asked for their drink orders. The table sat in a window that faced busy Frenchmen Street. "No thanks miss, I will just sip on my drink from the bar," said Imani.

"Sir would you like something else to drink? Maybe with your meal," said the waitress.

"Well, I will give you two a few minutes to review the menu. Please let me know if you have any questions.

I will be back shortly." The waitress left when no one responded.

"Surely, your day was not like mine," said David. Placing a finger to his mouth, he pressed the button on the phone. "What's up?"

Smiling at the beautiful man before her, Imani thought, *OMG (Oh my God) he is fine. Girl, focus. He has the prettiest, smoothest dark skin that flows to beautiful arms and legs. Focus. Focus. Maybe you can date this one for a minute. After all, he asked you to meet him last week after drinks and even called this morning after his run to remind you. He seems fine enough. A single black male with a job and no apparent baggage. Girl, he is wearing a nice button down shirt with silver cufflinks, nice slacks, nice shiny shoes, and a watch. He is a sexy, careful dresser; could he be a good lover?*

"Umm. Ummn. How was your walk yesterday?" he asked, refocusing the conversation.

"My walk was great. The girlies and I go on suicide strolls several times a week to just talk, vent, or refocus," said Imani.

"Suicide strolls?" said David.

"We jokingly call them that because of the length and pace of these walks," said Imani.

"They must be something else," said David.

Imani nodded and stared at the man sitting before her. *Girl, look at you having drinks with a fine ass man. Well not drinks but dinner with a man like this.*

His phone rang again.

"Excuse, me one more time," David said. "Yes mother, what's wrong? I'm having dinner with a friend. No, I will be there later this evening." He clicked off his phone and said, "Sorry for the interruption. Where were we?"

"We were talking about suicide strolls. Do you work out?" said Imani.

"Yeah, sure when I get a minute. Between the practice, my mom, and friend/family obligations I stay pretty busy," said David.

"I understand. Life can be pretty hectic at times. What do you do for fun?" said Imani.

"Sometimes, I go clubbing but, to be honest I'm getting a little old to be running the streets," said David.

The cell phone ringing broke into their conversation. "Excuse me, Imani, I need to take this call. Hi Mom. What do you need? You need dinner. What do you want? I'm at Snugs. Do you want a burger? Okay I will bring you a burger on the way home. Mom, I'm out with a friend and this is your fifth call. This is starting to get on my nerves. I'm trying to enjoy the company of a lady friend and you keep calling. Is there anything else? I will not answer this phone again." David smiled at the phone. "Mom, I will bring you a burger and loaded potato. I will see you before nine o' clock." David ended the call by placing the phone back on his waist. "Now where were we?"

The waitress appeared. "Are you guys ready to order? Ma'am?"

"I will have a bowl of gumbo and a glass of water," said Imani.

"Sir?" said the waitress.

"Shrimp remoulade appetizer, mushroom Swiss cheese burger with a loaded baked potato, another Crown and seven, and a Barq's Root beer with the meal," said David.

Imani and David shared the Shrimp remoulade while watching the people walk by up and down the strip. Wiping the remoulade sauce from her fingers, Imani asked David about his upcoming weekend plans.

"I normally go to both weekends of Jazz Fest, but I'm truly not feeling all the people and the heat. I just want to relax," said David.

"What? You afraid of a little Nawlins heat? Say it ain't so," said Imani.

David laughed at Imani. "I am going to have to admit I might be slowing down a tad bit, I don't want to do the heat."

"Well there are always the gospel and jazz tents. They are both set up for old timers like you ... afraid of a little heat," said Imani.

"Now you got jokes on our date?" said David.

They both smiled as the waitress sat their dinners on the table. Imani spooned gumbo into her mouth and prayed for no accidents. *Girlie women with big breasts do not order soup based meals with men they are trying to invite to personal private parties. The last thing you want is for him to see you as a slob. After all, you just barely got him to want to have dinner with you. You lucked up into a dinner invitation.* Moving the conversation in another direction, she asked, "How's your burger?"

"Great as always. Do you ever get the burgers here?" said David.

"Every blue moon, me and the girlies will split one between us," said Imani.

"One burger between all the ladies I see you here with?" said David.

"Well, everyone doesn't eat meat. We all are very conscious of our weight and calorie intake," said Imani.

"If you say so, but I know for sure me and my friends could never share one burger between us," said David.

Imani laughed at David. "Yeah, I guess you couldn't share a burger with your friends."

The waitress approached the table with a cordless phone. "Excuse me, sir, but is your name David?"

"Yes." "You have a call," said the waitress.

"Excuse me, Imani Hello. Who is this and what do you want? Mom, are you for real …you did not just call the restaurant. An emergency. What's wrong? Ok, Ok I will be on my way. I just need to order your food and say good night to my lady friend. I cannot believe you just called the restaurant. Yes, I did feel my phone vibrate, but I also told you where I was and what I was doing. Anybody else would just have waited for me to return their call," said David. David hung up the phone and gave it back to the waiting waitress.

"Imani, look I'm sorry but I need to cut our evening short. Do you mind taking the rest of your gumbo to go?" said David.

"Sure, David, it's no problem." Imani chewed on her lip, and then asked, "Is everything all right with your mom?"

"Yes. She just feels the need to control my life. She still has the need to mother me. She wants me to come home to put the trash out and put gas in her car," said David.

"Has she looked at you lately?" said Imani.

"Yep. I look at me, too. I am very well aware of my grown up status," said David.

"Well thank you for inviting me to dinner." Placing her left hand on his face, Imani said, "I had a great time." Imani kissed him on the cheek. "Thanks again."

Imani turned to look over her shoulder at the sexy attorney, David, for one more glance. Slowly waving bye to him, she said, "Good night." Damn, damn, damn! Another brother taken by his damn momma. "God, is there a regular brother anywhere in the city of New Orleans not taken by his momma?"

Shannon

Shannon rode the elevator to the third floor and slowly walked to her office. The last two weeks had been a whirlwind of action, movement, and changes. First, a job change from working the floor to working in human resources. Second, moving from a beautiful condo to a rental house in a private gated community. Three, leaving Derrick without a trace or clue of her status. *I would have paid good money to see his controlling ass face when he realized, I no longer lived in our condo. I still can't believe Derrick tried to play me like a cheap ass girlie.* Walking with a sexy flow and confident stride, Shannon pushed open the door to her office and scanned the day's workload. Corporate casual in linen denim colored slacks, multi-color tank, and lightweight jacket, Shannon scanned the list and decided all was well: A morning meeting to review company policy and procedures for new hires, followed by a working lunch and power point presentation.

Four hours into the day, today's list is almost complete. Shannon leisurely checked off tasks. *Now, to get finished to get out of here.* Placing the empty coffee cup on the table, Shannon focused on the people before her. Her presentation ended without event. Now, on to the task at hand ...interviewing people to work the floor at stores throughout the city.

Later, stepping through the door of her new place, and placing cleaning supplies on the counter, she said, "Girl, do you like this house and your current situation? Well, there is nothing we can do to change our current situation. It had gotten way too hot living with Derrick." Smoothing her pants over her butt, she told herself, "That man was trying to kill your looks and ass- sets. You know the rules and what momma would say. You need to keep it tight and pretty to land a beautiful and financially successful black man."

Shannon moved through the kitchen while preparing a light supper of Greek yogurt, sliced fruit, and sparkling water. Placing the yogurt, fruit, and a spoon on a square plate, she picked up the phone to call Candy.

"Hey. What's up?" "I'm beyond busy at the moment," said Candy.

"Candy, what are you up to now?" said Shannon.

"Well if you must know, I'm low riding in Shelby to see the comings and goings at Justin's house. I will not have a man ignore me. After all, mirror, mirror tells me every day that I am the sexiest of all."

"Candy, for real ... are you serious? You are outside that man's house watching his moves?" said Shannon.

"Well... not his every move. I'm just trying to see if some woman is dealing with him. Do you know Justin has ignored my calls?" said Candy.

Shannon looked at the phone and asked, "Candy, can you hear yourself? Do you even like this man?"

Twisting her face and looking at the phone, Candy screamed into the speaker, "Girlie be real. I'm not concerned about liking him. I will not be ignored by a man. If one man ignores you, it's the beginning of the end. I'm fine for life. Anyway, enough about me. How do you like your new house?" said Candy.

"It's okay. I just finished preparing me a light dinner. I miss Derrick, but I am looking forward to finding a new friend," said Shannon.

"Have you met anyone interesting at work?" said Candy.

"No, just a bunch of corporate types. I miss working the Shannon system on the floor. I just need to find a way to meet new people and focus on new gains," said Shannon.

"Well, I need to say goodnight. It is too hard ducking under the dash of my car while trying to watch a house," said Candy.

"Good night, friend," said Candy.

"Good night and be careful out there," said Shannon.

Pressing Alexis' name on the phone, Shannon dialed another friend, thinking, *Everyone can't be tied up and unable to talk. Alexis and Imani should be good to pass some time as neither of them have a man.* "Hey, what's up with you?"

"Umm, friend, I'm slightly busy. Is everything okay with you?" said Alexis.

Shannon stared at the phone in disbelief. "Yeah, I'm good. Why can't you spare a few minutes."

"To be honest I had just taken a bath and was about to go to sleep. I had a rather long day, and tomorrow I have another, so, I need some extra rest," said Alexis.

"I just needed to share about my job. I miss working the floor and flirting with men. Girlie, how am I going to work my show working in human resources?" said Shannon.

"Shannon, you are lucky to have that job. The drama with you and Derrick was a beast. Did you forget he came on your job to deal with you?" said Alexis.

Lying across the sofa and twirling a strand of hair between her fingers, Shannon replied "No! I didn't forget."

"Sounds like you have to stop tripping over there. You will meet another man. Shannon, what do you want?" said Alexis.

"You know what I want. I want a brother to take me out, buy me goods, pay for services, and spoil me rotten," said Shannon.

"Watch it, friend. Do you know what you just described?" said Alexis.

"I described the man-woman dynamics. All men pay women to give them services, mainly sex. I just put it out there. Girl, I'm getting older and need to secure a sponsor soon. What am I going to tell my mother?" said Shannon. "She was so disappointed when I moved from the condo. She thought it was blown way out of proportion with the police and stuff," said Shannon.

"You can start by telling her you love yourself enough not to stay in a bad situation. Shannon, enough about what your Moms wants, what you want?" said Alexis.

"Friend, didn't you hear me? I want a sugar daddy."

Shaking her head from side to side, Alexis said, "Girl, I'm tired and don't feel like processing tonight. Promise me you will think about your true desires."

"Goodbye."

"Goodnight, Alexis," said Shannon. Click. Shannon returned the phone to the charger.

Damn, Damn, Damn! Nobody to talk with, Candy is low riding in Shelby and Alexis is tired from work. It's only eight-thirty. How my friends trying to go to bed before ten? I guess I should just go to bed too.

Entering the closet to select an outfit for tomorrow, she thought, *Another day, another boring meeting on policy and procedures. I don't know how people do it. I hate working in human resources. I miss working the floor and flirting with fine ass men. Girlie, you got to find a new sponsor.*

Lillian

"Jared!" Lillian yelled through the house. "I know your bitch ass is here. Jared. Where are you, bastard?"

"Lillian, I'm sitting right here in my chair like always. What ... your little friends done gassed you up with courage? So now, you going to walk into my house calling me names," said Jared.

"No, Bitch ass Negro. My friends didn't gas me up. I just dropped the girls off at my parents for a visit. I decided it was time for us to face whatever this is we are doing," said Lillian.

Jared looked at Lillian. "I don't know what you are talking about. Anyway, lower your voice. I am trying to watch my show. A brother got to have a little TV time."

Running to the chair, Lillian punched Jared in the jaw. "Bitch ass Negro. You had a heffa low riding your lap in front my girls and our family and friends? Do you know how embarrassed I have been for the last few weeks? Everyone I know looks at me with pity. It's embarrassing to enter into rooms and everyone gets quiet. Your ass at my party…letting your woman feed you. Jared did she have to come to my party? My party? It was supposed to be a special day for me? What's wrong? Why I can't have one special day! Damn, Jared my party in-front our families?" said Lillian.

Turning to face the screaming Lillian, Jared said, "Look... are you done? You see I'm watching my show and I am peaceful. Get out of here with that shit, girl. You know I didn't desire to be with you anymore. When was the last time I touched you? I don't fuck you anymore. When the last time you saw my dick? Come on Lillian, when was that?" said Jared.

Lillian threw a full bottle of Crown Royal at his head. Splash!

"Bitch, are you crazy?" said Jared.

"I'm not crazy! I figure you won't touch me, so I will touch your shit. One of us is going to have their way. I will not have a husband who embarrasses me in front my family and children," said Lillian.

"Bitch! You better stop before I drag your ass out my house," said Jared.

"You must be confused. All your fucking and tricking to other women has removed a few brain cells. Bitch, I'm your wife and mother of your children. This is our home. I will not be moved and my girls will not have any interruptions to their childhood. Jared, do you know I have seen you many times with your woman ... or should I say women? The casino? Club? Dinner? Jared, you take them to some of my favorite spots. Places you been stopped taking me. What's up with that shit? Negro, are you going to answer me?" said Lillian. She picked up another bottle of liquor and tossed it at his chest. Splat! Girlie good throw, full body contact.

"Bitch, are you crazy?" yelled Jared.

"Yep, got your attention now," said Lillian.

"Lillian, you need to stop before I lose myself. I see your ass is a little spastic right now, so I will give you some space. If you throw another bottle of my liquor I will beat you the fuck up!" said Jared.

Caressing the lip of another bottle of liquor, she taunted, "Let me see … I got a good one. You do love your Hennessey?"

Screaming across the room Jared yelled, "What do you want"?

"I want respect in my home and a husband that doesn't date," said Lillian.

"Well, you can't have that. I enjoy going out with other women. I told you I didn't want a party here. You insisted on having a party so I figured my wishes are not respected, neither will yours be. Now, as for my women, that's my business. Do you have a house and children?" asked Jared.

"Yes," said Lillian.

"Isn't that what you wanted?" said Jared.

"Yes," replied Lillian.

"What's your problem? Aren't you raising your girls inside a marriage? Do you guys not live in a house in uptown New Orleans?" said Jared.

"Yes we do," said Lillian.

"Well, I see no problems. You have everything you said you wanted when we were dating," said Jared.

"Jared, this is not the life I wanted and you know it," said Lillian.

"I know nothing of the kind. I am very happy here. I enjoy my girls and our marriage," said Jared.

"Jared, how can you do this? I love you? You know I wanted more for my girls. This is not a marriage. I thought you were my friend? Jared I love you. Love you. How can you do this to us? Our girls? Jared I don't understand this. Jared I pray for us every day. I saw the way you caressed that woman in the casino. You had somebody different at my party. Jared how many women are you dating?" said Lillian.

"Lillian, you need to get a grip. I been doing this. I don't think you can handle the truth. Make this the last time you throw things at me. Next time you get this bold, I will hurt you. You will be very sorry you ever crossed me. Do you hear me?" said Jared.

"Yeah, bitch ass Negro. I hear you. Do you hear me? I will not be second. My God handles all things. I will not be abused by you and your women. I want a real marriage between a man and one woman. That one woman happens to be me, Lillian. My whole childhood my Moms was a lonely widow. I would rather raise my girls alone than to have them think our relationship is a marriage. Do you hear me, Jared? I have more than enough witnesses to your behavior. After all, our family and friends saw you playing lover boy at my birthday party," said Lillian.

Caramel Crème

Ringing the bell before using his key, Shane called, "Shay where you at? Shay, Shay! I know you're home. I saw your car in the driveway. Oh my God. Don't tell me you locked up with your husband in the middle of the day. Shouldn't you guys be past the honeymoon stage? "Shay?" said Shane.

"Boy, you about to raise the dead with all that yelling. I'm fine. I was just in the back." Reaching up to kiss and hug her brother, Shay asked, "What's up with my brother? You getting cold feet before your wedding now? What's got you coming to see me in the middle of the day?" said Shay.

Annoyed at his sister's comment, Shane twisted his face. "No I'm not afraid or scared to get married. I see this marriage as what it is. I love Nicole, but I'm in love with Candy. She makes my heart race whenever we are together."

"You mean she used to make your heart race? Right?" said Shay.

"Nope, I meant what I said. I recognize marrying Nicole Charbonnet will help my political career. She just doesn't do anything for me sexually or physically. I know she holds political power and status," said Shane.

"Who the hell is Candy?" said Shay.

"She is a woman I've been seeing for maybe a year or so," said Shane.

Pouring a glass of wine and placing it on the counter, Shay said, "Brother, are you being real? What are you going to do? Have you told her you are getting married? Shane, our parents will have a fit … not to mention Nicole's parents … if some ghetto houchie momma jumps out the shadows at your wedding. Shane?"

"Girl, take a sip of your wine and calm down. Candy would never do all that," said Shane.

"Shane, how can you say that? Is this lady in love with you? Did she start this relationship knowing she was a jump off?" said Shay.

Laughing at his sister's theatrics, he said, "Girl calm down. Candy is cool."

"What does she look like?" said Shay.

Shane mimicked his sister's hand gestures and replied, "Beautiful."

"Boy, does Dad know about this?" said Shay.

"Nope, I'm starting to feel bad for sharing with you. We have always been best friends but now I'm not sure," said Shane.

"Well, what do you want? I'm a girl. A girl with girl feelings. I would bust my husband in the head if he had a woman while we were dating," said Shay.

Shane said, "Have you forgotten? You married a man that was dating … what … five or six other women?"

"Okay, okay he was a hot boy. But, you are my brother. How are you willing to hurt Nicole?" said Shay.

"I'm not worried about Nikki, she will be okay regardless. Our relationship is cool. I just can't fathom my Candy girl with another man. She will no longer let me in her bed; the shit is driving me crazy. All day I'm thinking about having sex with her. I think Nikki might have a slight idea there is someone else," said Shane.

"What makes you think that?" said Shay.

"Well, she has been questioning my whereabouts more and she has been on edge," said Shane

"Boy, I doubt she knows you are messing over her. Every woman gets nervous before her wedding. I dreamed about my wedding for years before it happened, so as it approached I was so concerned about every detail," said Shay.

Shay took another huge gulp of wine. "Brother what are you going to do?"

Shane laughed at his sister. "I'm going to enjoy my Candy and marry Nicole. Candy is cool."

"Ok, brother … are you guys practicing safe sex?" said Shay.

Spitting out his drink, he said, "What?"

"What nothing …we are both grown. I know you must be getting down with this Candy woman. What about Nikki? Political career? If Candy gets pregnant, what are you going to do? Secrets don't remain secrets for long?" said Shay.

"I'm not worried about any babies. Candy and I practice safe sex. If we were going to have a child, it would have happened by now. Shay, we have had unpro-tected sex. I got caught up a few weeks ago, we went so hard. Damn, I need to ask Candy about her cycle," said Shane.

"Boy do you realize you are getting married in two weeks? Let me see the part of the vows you must have forgotten. To forsake all others?" said Shay.

Shane sipped more wine. "I didn't forget. I just enjoy my Candy."

"Why didn't you propose to Candy if she was all that?" said Shay.

"Well, I had already asked Nicole to marry me before I started dealing with Candy," said Shane.

"You have been engaged for almost two years."

"I've been with Candy almost the whole time," said Shane.

Shaking her head and draining the last of the wine from the goblet, Shay said, "Boy your wedding is going to be a sweet mess. Candy, right? You might want to let security know to be on alert."

"Girl, stop being so dramatic. Candy will not stir any mess. She loves me. She knows my heart. More than that I know her heart," said Shane.

Shay continued to shake her head. "If you say so, brother."

Imani

mani slowly began the suicide stroll while waiting on Candy and Shannon to play catch up, stopping at Candy's parked Shelby to stretch. *Wonder where she is? The car is warm but, no Candy insight.* The lake was full of waves and turbulence. *I'm starting to feel like the lake... full of motion, but no action.* Waving at the approaching figure, she said,"Hey girlie. How you feeling today?"

Shannon waved back to her friend. "I'm good just adjusting to my new job and not having a man. I'm still working the Shannon system. Where is Candy?"

Turning to face Shannon, she added, I don't know. I just stopped at her car to stretch. I thought maybe she was in the front, but I looked inside ... no Candy and the door is locked," said Imani.

"Knowing Candy like I do, she must have seen a fine ass potential sponsor and started her run early," said Shannon.

"Imani is everything okay with you? I mean an extra suicide stroll in the middle of the week? What's up with you?" said Shannon.

"I don't really want to be walking but I went to a spin class yesterday and everything hurts. I swear, who knew a bike could hurt your butt, couch, thighs, and everything below the waist," said Imani.

Raising her hands to her face, Shannon, smothered her laugh. "Girlie, you didn't know spin was a beast?"

"No, nobody ever said spin would put that kind of pressure on my couch. If I wanted pressure like that I would have had sex," said Imani.

"Umm girl, come on let's stretch and start walking," said Shannon.

"First, Alexis was out here taking an extra stroll with Candy, now you are taking one. How is your love life?" said Shannon.

"What love life?" said Imani.

"Come on, it can't be that bad. Breathe in through your nose and out through your mouth. If you get your breath together, we can step up our pace. Nothing like a good pace to burn a few extra calories. If you are willing to try spinning maybe you will try jogging. What do you think Imani?" said Shannon.

"I think I'm going to focus on getting a fourteen minute mile and walking the whole suicide stroll at that pace. Girl, come on. I can't run. I'm a voluptuous girlie with curves and breasts," said Imani.

"I don't know. Alexis was out here running and she has curves too," said Shannon.

"Well, I will call our girl and see what's up? She has been strange lately," said Imani.

"What do you mean?" said Shannon.

"Hey ladies," said Candy.

"Hey." The friends spoke together.

"Hey girlie," said Shannon.

"About time you two slow pokes catch up," said Candy.

"What are you doing sitting on a bench?" said Imani.

"I just felt so tired all of a sudden. I saw the most amazing man running earlier. So you know me. I had to go for a run, catch his pace, and get them digits," said Candy.

Rising up from the bench to stretch, she said, "Wow I'm dizzy. Let me stretch for a second. Placing her foot on the bench, Candy reached over to touch her feet.

"Is everything all right, Candy?" said Shannon.

"Yeah, you know me. I've been busy. I didn't get much sleep last night. Then on top of that, I had a busy day at the hospital. We had several nurses' call in and I had to work a floor, then I was determined to catch that man earlier," said Candy.

"Sounds like you need to walk with us and slow down. Candy, you need to take care of yourself," said Shannon.

"You know we need our Candy girlie in the circle to keep us entertained," said Imani.

Candy's legs and stomach burned from her previous pace. Imani focused on breathing in through her nose and out the mouth. Shannon mentally started making a plan for meeting a new Orca. The girlies finished an extra suicide stroll in record time.

Stopping at Candy's car the ladies said, "Goodnight."

"Goodnight girlies," said Candy.

"Candy, get some rest. You look pale tonight," said Imani.

The next day, Imani greeted her client. "Good morning, Shay."

"Good morning, Imani."

"I'm sorry for all the calls but I'm in chaos. I can't believe what is happening to me," said Shay.

"Ms. Waters, your behavior in the office is out of control. Counseling Connections is a professional counseling office with a pleasant atmosphere. We can't have a client calling thirty times in one day and harassing the other clients in the lobby to cancel their appointment so you can have one. Do you understand?" said Imani.

"Yes, I understand," said Shay.

"Tell me what's going on now?" said Imani.

"My brother came to see me. He shared with me that he has a woman. A woman. My beautiful brother has a woman. I feel so bad, I like his fiancé. How am I supposed to face her knowing he has another woman that he claims he loves? How can he love her? He is about to marry a different woman," said Shay.

"Can you explain to me why you were blowing up all the phones and lobby because your brother has a woman?" said Imani.

"Don't you get it? If my brother has a woman then every man has a woman. That's why my husband no longer does what I tell him to do," said Shay.

"Do you hear yourself?" said Imani.

"Of course, I hear myself. It's all I can think about. My brother has a woman. He is planning a political career and dating a woman named Candy. What is he thinking?" said Shay.

"Shay can you refocus? People come to counseling to talk about themselves and their personal goals," said Imani.

Leaning forward with her elbows on her thighs, Shay spoke to Imani. "Don't you get it? My brother has a woman, so surely my husband does too!"

"Are you seriously judging your husband by your brother's behavior?" said Imani.

"Yes. Oh my god … this is why my husband doesn't touch me. He has a woman. He will not live in my house and have a woman too. I make the most money so I should have the ultimate say. He will not disrespect me in my own home," said Shay.

Imani quietly took notes as Shay ranted about money, men, and control.

"Shay do you know anyone with a healthy relationship?" said Imani.

"Of course, I know people with healthy relationships. I have one. My parents have one. My brother and Nicole have one," said Shay.

"Shay, you came here today all upset about your brother correct?" said Imani.

"Yes, I'm worried about him. Nicole loves him. She wants the best for him and her," said Shay.

"Have you ever considered what a man might want or think is the best for him?" said Imani.

"I know what is best for my husband …just like Nicole knows what's best for my brother. I'm just going to tell her," said Shay.

Pulling her glasses from her face, Imani asked, "Shay, are you honoring your brother or yourself with this drama in my office? Do you really think your brother's fiancé does not know about the woman in his life?"

Shay refocused on Imani and said, "I don't know. All I keep thinking is she should know about this woman."

"Why are you here now, Shay?" said Imani.

In a forced whisper through clinched teeth, "I don't know," said Shay.

Shannon

Yoga pants and tiny tee hit the floor with the closing of the front door. *Great class and run but we need to hit the spot if I'm ever going to find a new Orca. I need a man to complete me. I need a friend to pamper and spoil me. I can't wind up like Imani and Alexis with only work as company. I mean, those two girlies never have a man. It is pathetic how Imani dates one hopeless Momma's boy after another. I cannot wind up hanging with that crew.*

Shannon started water for a quick shower. Hot water flowed from the tap along with lemongrass shower gel from a decorative decanter. *Time to get going and out to find a new sponsor,* Shannon thought, stepping out of the shower to face a cloudy mirror. Wipe, wipe. Okay girlie, breasts are full and no rolls of fat to be seen. A cute patch of well-trimmed hair. Turn. Arms up. Looking over my shoulders at me in the mirror. Girlie, looking good. You need to lose maybe five more pounds. Another week of fruit and Greek yogurt, with five to six mile runs, and the body will be in top shape. Nothing like running to get your stomach, calves, and butt in perfect shape.

Drying off with a fluffy white towel and then using it as a cover, Shannon picked up the phone to call Candy.

"What you doing?" said Shannon.

"Nothing … about to hit the streets to see King," said Candy.

"Who the hell is King?" said Shannon.

"You remember. He is the deejay I've been flirting with for weeks. I call him King and he calls me Sandals. I met him slow sipping one night in a hammock. He was so sexy and charming. I can't wait to see where this flirtation goes. Every time I walk into the club he mixes, Candy, I want Candy, or I'm talking about Candy into the mix. Girlie, he makes me feel like a real celebrity. I like the way he gets down with me."

"Humph, at least somebody has someone treating them good," said Shannon.

"What's wrong with you?" said Candy.

"I'm sick of this house and my job. I miss working the floor and meeting new men. Derrick had gotten a bit out of control, but I don't think I should have been so drastic in changing so much about myself," said Shannon.

"Did somebody forget; he tried to slam your face through the floor on that very front end you miss so much? Girl, you can't have that kind of drama in the grocery store. Women go there to fantasize about the man they are cooking for. How you going to bring ghetto reality to the grocery store? We both know the grocery store and soaps are the places where all dreams come true," said Candy.

"I know girl, but I'm bored and need a new sponsor," said Shannon.

"Need?" said Candy.

"Okay correction, I want a new sponsor. Girl I got to use my skills and this beautiful trophy body before it starts to break down. I was just admiring myself in the mirror. My runs and Greek yogurt are doing the trick. I have no visible rolls of fat. A girlie can never be too careful. One bad break-up will damn you to a life of no men or even worse, bitch boys," said Shannon.

"Bitch boys?" said Candy.

"Yes, the men Imani dates," said Shannon with a laugh.

"Whatever girl, you need to stop, get dressed, and meet me at the club. I will be there. Check the deejay booth. I got to work this dress. I need to make King weak. If it's a good night Justin will be there again," said Candy.

"Justin?" said Shannon.

"Derrick must have fried your brain. The man whose house I've been passing by. The brother who has been ignoring me. A few weeks back, remember I told you I saw his friends out and modeled my dress? Tonight I hope to see all the men and work my show. What Candy wants, she gets. I will be looking for you girl," said Candy.

"All right. Maybe I can find me some action at the club too. Maybe the deejay can work some Shannon magic. If my friend does well he might even play my song," said Shannon.

"Hurry up … the night is young. Please dress to impress," said Candy.

Candy

Mirror, Mirror on the wall who is the sexiest Candy of all?

Of course, it's me. One more quick check and it's time to hit the club. King won't know what hit him. Chanel liner to make my lashes extra-long, eggplant, mocha, and vanilla eye shadow, Mac pressed powder, mocha lip glass. Check. Mist of Lovely perfume. Check. Crème colored backless halter top with a matching pencil skirt. Check. Four-inch coral BCBG strappy back zip-up sandals. Check. Mirror, Mirror this girlie is hot. Candy, girl you have struck a beautiful, chic, sassy balance tonight. King won't know how to handle the fire you will start. Check. Candy is about to find herself a new King tonight.

"How can I help you?" said the bartender.

"I will have a lemon drop with a sugar rim and a crown and seven," said Candy.

"Umm." A gulp of perfectly blended lemon flowed down Candy's throat. "Oh Sugar, this is delicious. Can you fix me another? I can't have just one of these," said Candy.

"Okay another lemon drop is on the way," said the bartender.

Walking with a slow sensual stride to the deejay booth, Candy took another sip of lemon drop. "Where is my theme music? A girlie could get a complex about stuff like that," said Sandals.

King smiled as Candy placed a drink on his booth. Kissing King on the cheek, she said, "A sexy king deserves a royal drink."

Candy took another sip of her drink, motioned to the bartender, and mouthed, "Two more."

King took a swallow of his drink, and scanned Candy from head to toe. "Girl you are looking very sexy tonight. What you trying to do, kill a brother? I mean you have on some very sexy shoes along with a backless shirt. If I didn't know better I would say you were plotting on me."

Candy swallowed more lemon drop and let the compliments wash over her body. Taking another sip of her drink, a low moan escaped Candy's lips.

"King, your words and this drink are doing wonders for my body. I might need to find out your name and invite you home. I am still curious how you found out my name. When we left the hammocks, I was still Sandals." Raising her foot to King, Candy asked, "Do you like my sandals tonight?"

"Girl, those are most certainly some serious sandals," said King.

"Umm. Well sir, my shoe game must be on point."

"Yes, Candy, your shoe game is exceptional."

"King, I don't want to interfere with your set. I will be at the bar. One of my girlfriends is meeting me here."

Placing a fresh drink on the booth, she told him, "Here is another royal drink for my future King."

Shannon wrapped her arms around Candy's shoulders. "Hey, girlie. You sitting at the bar all by yourself," said Shannon. "You are working that dress. Damn. I would have worn a hotter outfit if I knew you were throwing down like this." Pulling Candy up by the hand to spin her friend around, she added, "Girl you looking good. And those shoes are some bad mama jammers. That's some shoes right there."

Laughing at her friend, Candy could only shake her head. "Girl you are too much. I like your outfit too."

"Well friend, I didn't have much prep time so I threw on a maxi dress and some bangles. I wanted to create a symmetrical interest at the wrist. I want to draw a few potential sponsors if possible. It's hard out here on a girlie with no man," said Shannon. Shannon turned around in the bar stool and looked around the club. She asked, "Any hot men in the spot?"

"Not that I have noticed. I just came here to work King a bit. A girl has to prime a sponsor before lowering her traps. You know the rules. Nothing like a little honey and sugar to make a man lose his mind." Placing a hand to her mouth and blowing a breath, she said, "King is a goner."

"Work that show, friend," said Shannon.

Pulling the last of the lemon drop from the martini glass, she said, "Are you ready to hit Therapy Wine Bar?"

"Don't you normally go to the Wine Loft?" said Shannon.

"Yep, but tonight I want to go to a different spot. A sexy birdie told me that Justin is having a set over there for his birthday."

"Are we invited or are we crashing?" said Shannon.

"Girl, we are officially crashing therapy," said Candy.

Candy and Shannon giggled together. "Girlie we should have invited Alexis and Imani. They are our resident therapy buddies," said Shannon.

"They would like going to Therapy Wine Bar," said Candy.

Later, Candy and Shannon swayed to the beat and moved through the wine bar's crowd. The sounds and previous drinks started to relax Candy's body.

"Candy, the atmosphere in here is nice. We must come back here with the girls," said Shannon.

"Damn, you spoke too soon. Do you see that bitch sitting on the bar holding court like he ain't married to our friend?" said Candy.

"Where?" said Shannon.

Lifting her right hand, she pointed to the edge of the bar. Candy motioned in the direction of Jared. "Do you see him?"

"No," said Shannon.

"I swear you must be blind. Look at the man with the lime green polo shirt. I swear he is never that clean when he is with Lillian"

"Well, we can always wait for his ass to go to the bathroom and beat that ass," said Candy.

"Candy, aren't we a little old for that shit?" said Shannon.

"I don't feel old. Do you feel old?" said Candy.

"Me, myself. I'm not old. Did you see me in this dress tonight? I see you in that halter. Old broads can't rock clothes like us," said Shannon.

Tapping a fresh drink to Shannon's, she added, "Girlie you right about that." Strolling to the table with purpose and mischief, Candy thought, *Lawd have mercy. Marcus. Check. Justin. Check. Caramel Crème. Check. Nicole. Check. Time to have some fun. Girlie, you better work this moment for all it's worth.* "Shannon darling, I'm going say hello over there to Justin. Please watch and learn. You might even want to film this for the girlies."

"Film what?" said Shannon.

"Oh, you will know exactly what to film," said Candy.

Candy plopped down in the center of Justin's lap, swinging her legs to the other side to show off her sexy shoes and curves. Kiss. Kiss. She kissed Justin's cheeks on both sides like the French do. "Bonjour Justin. Greetings everyone, to the people around the table. Marcus how you feeling today?" said Candy.

"I'm good, Candy. How you doing?" said Marcus.

"You know this Candy girl is great. Your friend keeps me doing just fine," said Candy.

Extending her hand to the couple seated across from Justin, she said, "Hi. My name is Candy. Are you two friends of my Justin?"

"Yeah, Justin and I go way back. He is actually serving as an usher at my wedding," said Nicole.

"Wedding? You don't say. Who are you marrying?" said Candy.

"Oh let me introduce you to my fiancé, Shane."

"Hi Shane. Nice meeting you," said Candy. Waving over her shoulder to Shannon, she said, "Girl come join us."

Standing and twirling around, to allow everyone to see her sexy outfit and killer shoes, Candy pulled up two chairs. "Justin, you must tell me about the happy couple."

"Nikki and I go way back to middle school. She used to date my cousin but, she is marrying my college friend Shane."

"Make me know Shane from college," said Candy.

"Candy, you don't know this man from Xavier?" said Justin.

"Nope. Can't say that I do. Leaning forward and blowing air kisses at Shane, she said, "Sorry love. I don't remember you," said Candy.

"It's cool, Candy. No problems," he replied.

Stepping through the wine bar's doors, Candy scanned all around. *A girlie can never be too careful, flexing in front of two sexually charged men is always dangerous.* Sitting behind the wheel of her car, Candy pulled her cell phone and dialed Shannon. "Girl, call me when you get home and set the alarm."

"Later girlie."

"Later," said Shannon.

There was pounding on the door. "Candy, open the damn door!" said Caramel Crème.

Opening the door and standing in the entry, she said, "Greetings." "Caramel Crème … funny meeting you here. I don't remember inviting you here tonight," said Candy.

"Candy that shit tonight was not funny or cute. I am marrying Nicole in a few days," said Caramel Crème.

"Are you trying to tell me something or tell yourself something, Mr. Crème?" said Candy.

"Candy this shit is not cool," said Caramel Crème.

Moving to the side to allow Caramel Crème to enter, Candy walked to the sofa. "I don't see the problem with me trying to date someone. Justin is a very nice man. He finished school. Check. Single. Check. Has no baggage. Check. No kids. Check. Wants to fuck me. Super-size. Check. I think he is a wonderful catch for a girlie," said Candy.

"Candy, are you seriously going to date a man in our circle?" said Caramel Crème.

"Yes. I plan to date and fuck Justin. Look. I want a man for me. I want a man to cook for me and open my legs for more than an occasional good time. Can you promise me something?" said Candy.

"Candy, you know what we have," said Caramel Crème.

Covering her mouth with a hand to stifle a yawn look, she said, "Shane I'm tired. But while you're here. I need to pee on a stick for you."

"Candy, what are you talking about, girl?" said Caramel Crème.

"What? Do I detect some panic in Mr. Crème?" said Candy, slowly walking to the bathroom to open a home pregnancy test. "I'm talking about little Caramel Crèmes. Did you forget we have gone raw a few times?" said Candy. "I'm talking about being pregnant. I have been so tired lately. The other day I could not finish my run. When was the last time you saw me, the Candy girl tired? Exactly," said Candy.

Caramel Crème's hands tightened into fists as he slowly crumpled into a chair. "Candy, you can't be pregnant," said Caramel Crème.

"Why not? We fuck? Check. We go raw? Check. Well ... seems simple enough there is a chance I'm pregnant," said Candy.

"Candy, you know what I mean. I plan to run for office and marry Nicole Charbonnet."

"Oh well, you will just have to be a grown up and tell little Ms. Precious that you put me in an attic to protect her." Candy pointed her finger at Shane's chest. "How you going to protect her now?"

Picking up the pregnancy test from the counter, Candy showed the results to Caramel Crème. "It's positive. Aren't you happy?" said Candy.

Shifting in his chair, Caramel Crème started to devise a plan. "Candy, do you want this baby?" said Caramel Crème.

"What?" said Candy.

"Candy, you heard me. I need to know, if you want to be a mother at this time?" said Caramel Crème.

Stumping to the door and pulling it open, "Shane, get the fuck out!" screamed Candy.

"Baby, wait up, I'm thinking. I need to make this right for you and Nicole," said Caramel Crème.

"Get out," replied Candy.

Thursday

mani turned into the hallway to snake through all the people. "Hey girlies."

"Hi Imani," said Alexis.

"Where is everyone?" asked Imani. Plopping into an empty chair, she said, "Looks like everyone in NOLA came to catch the set tonight."

"Candy is working magic at the bar and Shannon just parked across the street," said Alexis.

"Well, looks like Thursday is ready to begin. Yeah everyone is here tonight. I took the liberty to order you some Moscatini's. I figured a sweet tini might be a good thing," said Candy.

Sitting down at the last available chair, Shannon said, "Hi girlies."

"Girlie you ran up in here, but did you stop and glance at Private Joy's word of the week? The word of the week is honesty," said Lillian.

"No I didn't get a chance," said Shannon.

"The word of the week, honest to speak in candid, truthful and straight forward manner," said Alexis.

"Anyway ladies, please raise your glasses and toast to honesty. We all know about being honest. Let's toast to telling the truth and loving each other despite our personal challenges," said Imani.

Clink. Clink. Clink. Clink. Clink.

Tapping the glass to get everyone's attention, Lillian cleared her throat. "Ummn. Ummm. Girlies I need to be honest with you all. I love my husband, but I don't know what to do. Jared is my everything. I have been so afraid of being alone that I have let this man walk all over me. I threw his prized liquor at him the other night. That Negro didn't get mad until I threw three of his precious bottles at him," said Lillian.

"All I want to know is, did you make contact?" said Alexis.

"Contact?" said Lillian.

"Yes. Contact," said Alexis. "Did you rap him in the center of his head with one of those bottles?" said Alexis.

Taking another sip of her Moscatini, Lillian smiled back at the eyes on her. "Sorry ladies I didn't hit him in the head. I did throw a bottle at his chest. And yes, it did break. That was the only thing that made him mad," said Lillian.

Rubbing her hands on her face, Candy held back another yawn. "Sorry girlies I've been so tired," said Candy.

"What's wrong with you?" said Shannon.

"I'm just tired and having morning sickness," said Candy.

Pulling her glass from her hand, Imani asked, "Morning sickness?"

"Yes ladies. I'm pregnant for a man I've been seeing," said Candy.

"Does he know?" said Alexis.

"Yes, he is aware. After the club last night I was feeling super tired. The other day I couldn't finish my run, so it got me to thinking about my cycle. A girl does have to keep up with a few things," said Candy.

"How does he feel about this? How do you feel about this? What are your plans?" said Imani.

"Well he is scared and concerned. Tomorrow is his wedding. He plans to have a political career. Let's just say a baby might be a problem," said Candy.

"I'm going to need to need more than this Moscatini," said Alexis.

"I know that's right. I'm going to order a round of Snugly mojitos and a Sweet taste fruit punch for you," said Lillian.

"Girl, what are you going to do?" said Imani.

"I'm going to enjoy my child and change my lifestyle," said Candy.

"Girl, a baby changes your whole focus. Are you sure?" said Lillian.

"Yes, I'm sure," said Candy.

"Are you going to crash the wedding?" said Lillian.

"No. I'm not going to ruin that girl's special day. Most girls dream about their wedding," said Candy.

"To be honest, most women dream of having their husbands' first born," said Lillian.

"Too bad. She can have a part of the dream. She just can't have it all. If she wants to have the whole dream she needs to leave my Caramel Crème alone," said Candy.

"While we are confessing to each other. I must tell you girlies I hate my house and really miss working the floor. I want to meet a new man, and working a corporate casual setting in human resources is not working for me," said Shannon.

"We are aware," said Imani.

"Girl, give it a chance. You might just meet your prince in that office. Human resources touches every part of the company. You just might meet a new man," said Alexis.

"Yep, Yep. Let's toast on that, girlies," said Shannon. Clink.

Tapping the glass on its side, tap, tap, and tap. "Ladies, I have a friend. He is wonderful. I enjoy him. I like going on dates and the fact that he treats me like a princess," said Alexis.

Imani grabbed Alexis' arm. "Is he Mr. Text during the show?"

"Yes, I enjoy this man," said Alexis.

"What the freak is happening?" said Lillian. "Alexis has a man, Candy is pregnant, I tell Jared to get out, and Shannon is independent. Are we about to fall into the gulf?" asked Lillian.

"Friend calm down. You sound like you are hating on your girlies. We are just getting older and wiser," said Imani.

"Imani, what's new with you?" said Lillian.

"Nothing. I don't have a man, no sex buddy, and I have nothing to report. Damn, Damn, Damn. My life is boring with no hope of recovery. I want to have some action. Will I ever get some penis? Ladies, if I knew that last time I had sex was going to be the last time, I would have enjoyed it more," said Imani.

"Oh don't worry, he is coming. Let the ancestors work their show. It is good to avoid bumps and bruises. Enjoy life, live, and have some fun. When you least expect it he will knock you off your feet," said Alexis.

"Ummph. That's some kind of talk for you," said Candy.

"Like I said, I enjoy my friend," said Alexis.

"Nope be honest girlie. You love your friend," said Lillian.

Taking a big gulp of Remy Martin, Alexis said, "Yes ladies, I love me some Suga."

"Come on ladies, I need your help," said Lillian. "I love Jared and want my marriage to work. What should I do?"

"Lillian maybe you and Jared should go to counseling," said Imani.

"You two cannot come to Counseling Connections," said Alexis. "It would be a conflict of interest. We already have one crazy ass client. "Correction. Imani has one crazy ass client. While we are being honest, the whole office would appreciate you discharging little miss crazy," said Alexis.

"Alright, Alexis, must you bring work to drinks?" said Imani.

"Yep. As long as you have crazy disturbing the office staff," said Alexis.

Tap. Tap. Tap. Imani tapped her half-empty glass to the beat, signaling the end of another Thursday night. "Ladies, raise those glasses. To having wonderful girlies to share the ups and downs of life. I love you girlies. Let us pray for peace and love, the health of Candy's baby, and joy," said Imani. "Good night."

"Good night, Joe. See you next week," chorused a set of friends.

"Good night, ladies. See you next week."

Laughing as she approached the top of the steps at her house, Candy ran into Shane sitting there and spoke to him. "Good evening, Mr. Crème," said Candy.

"Hi Candy. How are you feeling?" said Caramel Crème.

"I'm good. Just a little tired," said Candy.

"Candy, girl, I love you but I am unprepared for a baby. Yesterday, I left without telling you how I really feel," said Caramel Crème.

"Shane, look. I'm tired and wanting to take a bath and go to bed. If you are coming, come on, if not, get to stepping so I can set the alarm," said Candy.

Pushing to his feet, and up from the steps at Candy's front door, Shane quietly pulled her into a hug. He placed his hand on her tight stomach. "I love you guys," said Shane. Shane picked her up and carried her to the over-sized giraffe print chair in the corner. Shane continued to rub Candy's stomach. "I love you my Candy girl." Caramel Crème pulled his cell phone from the case and texted Nicole: "Nicole we need to talk. Sorry, but I can't do it! Shane."

Candy smiled at the man before her and thought, *Checkmate.*

Drink Menu

WHISKEY SOUR

- 1 ½ oz whiskey
- 4 oz sour mix

Combine whiskey and sour mix in a glass. Pour over ice. Garnish with a cherry and lemon wedge.

CHAMPAGNE PUNCH

- 2½ oz champagne
- 1 oz Jack Daniels
- 1 oz pineapple juice

Combine champagne, Jack Daniels, and pineapple juice and shake with ice. Garnish with a pineapple wedge.

WHITE WINE SPRITZER

- 2oz white wine
- 2 oz diet lemon lime soda

Mix equal parts wine and soda.

NAUGHTY SHIRLEY TEMPLE

- 2 oz gin
- 5 oz lemon lime soda
- 1oz grenadine syrup

Pour syrup, add ice, pour soda and top with gin. Garnish with a cherry.

CANDY APPLE MARTINI

- 2 oz vodka
- 2 oz apple schnapps
- 2 oz cranberry juice

Shake ingredients over ice to chill. Pour into martini glass. Garnish with an apple slice.

CARAMEL CANDY APPLE MARTINI

- 2oz vodka
- 2oz apple pucker

- 1oz cranberry juice
- 2tbs caramel syrup

Shake ingredients over ice to chill. Pour into a martini glass drizzled with caramel syrup. Garnish with apple slice drizzled with caramel.

LEMON DROP

- 4 oz lemon juice
- 2 oz vodka
- 1 tsp sugar
- 1 lemon wedge

Combine lemon juice, vodka, and sugar into a glass. Mix over ice to chill. Garnish with lemon wedge.

DIRTY MARTINI

- 3oz vodka
- 1 oz dry vermouth
- ½ oz olive juice

Shake ingredients and pour into a martini glass. Add olives.

RED ROYAL

- 2oz amaretto
- 2oz crown royal

- ½ oz cranberry juice

Mix ingredients together pour over ice into a highball glass.

GINGER MARTINIS

- 3 oz vodka
- 1 ½ oz Appleton rum
- 2oz ginger syrup
- ½ oz lime juice

Mix together and pour over ice into a martini glass. Garnish with a ginger candy and lime slice.

JACK DANIELS GINGER ALE

- 3oz ginger ale
- 2oz Jack Daniels

Mix together and pour over ice. Serve with lemon and lime garnish.

SWEET TASTE FRUIT PUNCH

- 2oz pineapple juice
- 2oz orange juice
- 1 oz fruit punch concentrate
- 1 oz lemon lime soda
- 1 fruit medley kabob

Combine ingredients and serve over ice. Garnish with fruit medley kabob

---

SNUGLY MOJITO

- 2 oz rum
- 2oz soda
- 1 oz lime juice
- Mint leaves
- Lime slices
- 2 sugar cubes

Stir all ingredients over ice. Serve with bits of mint leaves and lime mix into drink. Garnish with lime wedge.

Discussion Questions

1. What is a friend? Do you feel the ladies are truly friends? Do they support each other?

2. Do you feel any of the characters goes too far in the name of friendship?

3. What character is most like yourself or one of your friends?

4. Do you like Candy's nickname for Shane? (Caramel Crème) Why or why not?

5. Do you have a group of friends that you regularly go out with and discuss your respective lives? Why or why not?

6. What do you think of Lillian's behavior/relationship with Jared?

7. Should women put their friendships, their job, or their man first?

8. Do you think there is more to Alexis' desire to keep her relationship with Michael a secret?

9. Is there any reason a man should be allowed to mess over his partner?

10. What do you think of the Shannon system? Do you feel her mother was respectful to her daughter and her friends?

11. Would you consider having a relationship with a man like Jared, Michael, Derrick, Shane, King, David, or Corey?

12. Will Imani ever find a man? Will all her dates be with Mommas boys? Why do you think Imani draws unavailable men to her?

13. Which of the friends do you feel has a closer bond? Why or Why not?

14. What was your favorite adventure in this book?

15. Do you feel the characters understand love; love themselves, and the men they pursue?

16. Is Candy a stalker?

17. Do you have questions or curiosity about what will happen next to each of the characters?